Praise for
Emma's Journal

"I had tears in my eyes after reading the last page of my friend Ed Rowell's book *Emma's Journal*. Laced with hope, humor, and real-to-life honesty, this beautifully crafted novel shows the huge impact one person's life can make in this world. It exhibits the power of a life lived moment by moment for God."

—REBECCA ST. JAMES, singer, songwriter, and author of
Wait for Me

"*Emma's Journal* has the potential to reach out through pages of fiction to teach the love and forgiveness of God to people who may never intentionally pick up a Christian book. Forgiveness, acceptance of others, and a real relationship with God are communicated in a powerful yet nonreligious way. Ed so beautifully communicates through fiction that it is never too late to make needed changes in life and relationships—the choice is ours."

—NANCY ALCORN, president and founder of Mercy
Ministries of America and author of *Mercy Moves
Mountains* and *Echoes of Mercy*

"This little story holds a wonderful treasure for readers of all ages. When unassuming Emma Estes starts 'living on purpose,' she records her journey in a way that profoundly affects her corner of the world. *Emma's Journal* continues to speak softly, long after the final page is turned."

—ROBIN JONES GUNN, award-winning, best-selling author
of *Sisterchicks on the Loose!* and the Glenbrooke series

EMMA'S JOURNAL

A NOVELLA

EMMA'S JOURNAL

Ed Rowell

WATERBROOK
PRESS

EMMA'S JOURNAL
PUBLISHED BY WATERBROOK PRESS
2375 Telstar Drive, Suite 160
Colorado Springs, Colorado 80920
A division of Random House, Inc.

The characters and events in this book are fictional, and any resemblance to actual persons or events is coincidental.

ISBN 1-57856-724-6

Library of Congress Cataloging-in-Publication Data
Rowell, Edward K.
    Emma's journal : a novella / Ed Rowell.—1st ed.
        p. cm.
    ISBN 1-57856-724-6
    I. Title.
    PS3618.O874E46 2003
    813'.6—dc21
                                2003008735

Printed in the United States of America
2003—First Edition

10 9 8 7 6 5 4 3 2 1

For Melody and Meagan

Acknowledgments

I'm indebted to Charlene Armitage for first teaching me some sixteen years ago the power of goal setting using Luke 2:52. Along with her husband, Vernon, they have been mentors and confidants throughout our time in ministry. My wife, Susan, has served as my editorial advisor from the very beginning of this writing adventure, and I value her insights now more than ever. To Joel Mayes, Chantelle Smith, and Kristi Dustin, thanks for reading and rereading those rough, rough first drafts and having the vision to see potential in them. To Robin Jones Gunn and T. Davis Bunn, your teaching at the Glorieta Christian Writer's Conference was a catalyst for me finding the courage to begin and finish this book. To Chuck Walker, thanks for the use of your Jackson Hole cabin. And to the WaterBrook editorial staff who have guided me so well through this process—Ron Lee, Dudley Delffs, and Carol Bartley— thanks for not allowing my work to be publicly viewed without professional revision!

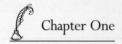

Chapter One

When it's time for me to go, I just want to know that my life made a difference. Lord, help me take advantage of every opportunity to touch others in ways that demonstrate your love.

—FROM EMMA'S JOURNAL, FOUND ON JANUARY 1ST

OF EVERY YEAR

E mma Estes fought her way out of her stroke's paralysis to verbalize her final words. Each word held profound possibility for those present, as well as for others she hadn't even met. Her eyelids fluttered, and she labored to form the syllables on her lips. Unfortunately, not a soul was listening.

Just moments before her family arrived, nurses had brought her from the emergency room and were getting her settled in the intensive care unit. Dr. Lloyd Foster just happened to be at the hospital making rounds when she was admitted. He had cared for Emma for the last half of her seventy-seven years. He had her chart in hand, though there was nothing in it he didn't already know. "Look," he told his senior nurse. "She's so tiny, you barely notice her under the blanket."

The nurse nodded and stroked Emma's forehead. Tubes and tape obscured the patient's worn face. "That white hair feathered around her head looks like a halo."

"I've never met a soul who fit one better," Dr. Foster claimed. "Most of us get more cranky with every birthday. Emma just got sweeter by the day."

The old woman's delicate hands were visible above the blankets. Attached to IV bags on stands, both were already bruising from the staff's many attempts to find her fragile, faint veins. Monitors and other equipment recorded every nuance of her bodily functions and relayed them to the ICU nurses at their station just a few feet away.

"I hope her family gets here soon," said the nurse. "I don't feel good about this."

"There is a time for everything, and a season for every activity under heaven…"

"What?"

"You're right. I think it's her time," said Dr. Foster.

As the gold Audi A6 left Overland Park and hit Interstate 35 north, it briefly hit seventy miles per hour. Emma's son was driving, his wife assisting. "Stuart, you need to watch your speed, dear. You can't afford to get another ticket."

Stuart Estes, known as Stu to everyone else, backed off the gas, bringing the car down to sixty-four. *I haven't had a ticket in eighteen years,* he replied, but the words stayed in his head.

He glanced over at his wife, Marilyn, a Rubenesque woman, tall of stature and full of figure. Her substantial dimensions were supported by a surprisingly dainty pair of feet clad in fine Italian pumps. As she pecked the buttons on her cell phone with a professionally manicured nail, her gold-and-diamond-covered fingers and wrists flickered in the sunlight. Even though it was the middle of an abnormally hot summer, Marilyn's designer suit betrayed not a bead of sweat on her.

As Marilyn waited for the call to go through, she pointed her left hand, which was holding a jumbo-size convenience-store mug of Diet Coke, at the dashboard and said, "Stuart, dear. Your thermostat says seventy-two. You know I like it on seventy. Take care of it, will you?"

Stu again answered only in his head, then brought the car's temperature down two degrees as her call connected.

"Tina? Hello, dear. Please connect me with Reverend Lamb. And, dear? This is an emergency." Being able to add that last line brought her immense pleasure.

She glanced at Stu while waiting for her pastor to pick up. "Sweetheart, we really must replace that suit. It's beginning to look dated. I'll call Tom at Coleman's and let him know you'll be coming in for a fitting. I think something with a more Italian cut would be... Oh, Pastor! I'm so glad you're in. Stuart and I are on our way to Liberty Hospital. We just received word that my dear mother-in-law was admitted. They think it's a stroke."

She took a sip of her drink while the pastor responded, her perfectly made-up face scowling at what she heard. "Later this evening? Why, I should think your grandson would excuse you from a silly birthday party for an emergency. Can we expect you to be at the hospital within the hour?" There was evidently some rationalizing on the other end. Marilyn pointed to the speed-ometer again.

"Why, thank you so much for your kindness, Pastor. We will look forward to your comforting presence. Blessings on you. Bye now."

After considering the consequences of speaking up, Stu did so. "Why should Pastor Lamb give up his grandson's birthday party to drive all the way across Kansas City for us? There's nothing he can do. He doesn't even know Mom."

"Well, he knows me, and since I'm a board member and his most committed volunteer, he'd better be there when I need him. That's why we pay him so well." Marilyn pursed her lips around the mug's built-in straw and decided whom to call next.

Stu just shook his head as they crossed first the state line, then the river into the Missouri side of Kansas City.

Skeeter Wilson had somehow managed to catch a ride in the ambulance with Emma, even though it was against policy. She had briefed first the ambulance crew, then the emergency-room doctor about what had happened.

"I was returning a videotape. Emma tapes that cooking show I like but don't get because I'm too cheap to pay for cable. She didn't answer the door, but I knew where the key was hidden and let myself in. There she lay, crumpled on the floor like a wad of tissue. That's when I called 911."

As the hospital staff went to work over Emma, someone with

a clipboard began asking Skeeter questions. Fortunately, she had possessed the presence of mind to grab Emma's purse off the counter before the ambulance left, and in it they found all the information they needed, including her son's phone number.

"I hardly know the man," Skeeter told the young woman filling out the admission forms. "Can you imagine that? I've lived across the street from Emma for more than twenty-five years, and I can count on one hand the times I've seen her children or their families. They ought to be ashamed of themselves."

As Stu drove through Gladstone on their way to the hospital in the bedroom community of Liberty, Marilyn made call after call, thrilled at the opportunity to alert everyone she knew to their crisis. She called their two sons, both away at college, and left messages on their voice mails. "Your grandmother is dying. You need to come home immediately. And don't forget to bring something decent to wear to the funeral."

Stu was physically as slight as his mother and psychologically made smaller by his survival strategy of living as a satellite that orbited at the edge of his wife's overwhelming gravity. He frowned at his wife's certainty of the outcome of his mother's hospitalization. But the fog of guilt he had been driving in came back immediately and almost smothered him as he considered the infrequent and insufficient time he had spent with his mother.

Marilyn often lamented—to anyone who would listen—the hardships she endured while caring for an elderly mother-in-law.

She saw it as a testimony to her willingness to suffer for righteous-ness' sake and evidence of her obedience to the biblical mandate to care for widows. "Pray for me to have the endurance to care for her," she'd whisper at prayer meeting. "I know it's a blessing to her; pray that I will be blessed as well."

For years Marilyn had insisted she take over Emma's financial affairs. Truth be known, the only reason Emma finally gave over these responsibilities and power of attorney was because it gave her daughter-in-law a reason to call her once in a while. "It makes her feel useful," she had told Skeeter.

In reality Emma had remained quite self-sufficient. "Mom," Stu had often asked, "what can we do for you?"

"I get along fine, Son. If you'll just make sure my grass gets mowed and find me a dependable repairman when something breaks down around the house, I'll be fine."

Both had tried on numerous occasions to get his mother to move to Johnson County, where they lived. Their weekly phone call usually ended with something like, "Mom, a nice retirement community would be so much better than your tiny old house. Beside, Claycomo isn't safe anymore. There are too many people moving in these days that you can't trust."

Emma fired back with determination in her voice. "I *like* my house. Claycomo is where my friends and my church are."

Claycomo was an aging community near the Ford motor plant where her husband had worked until his early death. Her house was like most on her street—sagging in the middle, with noisy plumb-ing and tiny closets, and a gravel driveway. But the little house on

Longfellow Street was continually filled with the aroma of home-cooked food and the laughter of friends. Her front porch served as the central meeting place for residents of her street to catch up on news, exchange garden vegetables, and hear an encouraging word.

Very few of her original neighbors remained, which was part of Stu's discomfort. As the community had changed, Emma had welcomed her new neighbors warmly—regardless of their ethnicity or status. Marilyn was embarrassed at her mother-in-law's simple life. It contrasted too much with her own.

Emma's final salvo in the ongoing battle reflected her one and only prejudice. "Why would I move into *Kansas* when everything I love is right here?"

The old interstate rivalry between citizens of this city on the border was ingrained deeply in Emma. She had no real reason to dislike the Kansas side of the city, except that she was from Missouri, which she pronounced "Mi-zoo-ruh." Everyone knew that the *real* Kansas City was in Mi-zoo-ruh. Kansas City, Mi-zoo-ruh, was home of the American League Royals, Emma's passion since they had debuted in Kansas City in 1969. Summer evenings weren't complete without a broadcast of the game competing with the locusts for attention. Kansas City, Mi-zoo-ruh, was home of the Country Club Plaza, where she and her friends had spent many a Thanksgiving evening watching the nation's first suburban shopping district be magically transformed as three hundred thousand Christmas lights illuminated the plaza. Kansas City, Mi-zoo-ruh, had more fountains than any other American city. Why anyone would move to Kansas was beyond Emma's comprehension.

As they neared the Liberty exit for the hospital, Stu's guilt peaked. The last time he had visited Emma was on Mother's Day. That was in May. This was August. He and Marilyn had picked up Emma after attending their church, delivered the obligatory flowers, taken her out for fried chicken at Strouds, then hustled her home so Marilyn could get back to church for evening services.

"I hope you had a good day, Mom," he'd said as he walked her to the door.

"Any day's a good day that I get to spend with one of my kids," she'd replied. "Come see me again soon."

Why didn't we give her more good days? he lamented as he pulled into the parking lot.

Uh-oh, thought the nurse as she saw Marilyn heading for the desk.

Though Marilyn had her standard smile on, her voice was crisp. "I'm Emma Estes's legal guardian. We want to see her physician immediately and get an update on her condition."

"I'm sorry, you just missed Dr. Foster. He's already left to go back to his—"

"I'm not here to listen to excuses, dear. Please pick up that phone and call him at once."

While the nurse engaged every diplomatic skill in her repertoire, Stu tried to call his sister. He had received permission to use his wife's phone, along with thorough instructions on how to use it properly without erasing her speed dial.

His sister's name was Judy. But Marilyn, when necessity demanded they mention Judy, preferred derogatory titles in place of her name. Marilyn was not particularly creative; most of her labels were predictable once you knew that Judy had married and divorced quite young, then gone through a string of unhealthy relationships, one of which resulted in the birth of a daughter out of wedlock.

The phone rang twice before Judy answered. "It's Mom," said Stu. "Probably a stroke. You need to get to Liberty Hospital as quick as you can."

While Marilyn continued her assault on the staff, Stu walked in and sat beside his mother's bed. As he watched her, he cried and swallowed lump after lump of regret.

Judy showed up quicker than anyone expected. Her home in Gladstone was not far, and she had been at the orthodontist's office with her daughter when she got the call. No one noticed her presence at first, a tribute to her fashion strategy of dressing to be invisible. Black knit pants and a long tunic top covered her thickening middle and broad hips. Her brown hair was short and in a style that neither required maintenance nor flattered her in any way.

Ashley floated in her mother's shadow. Marilyn never referred to this pretty twelve-year-old girl by name either, preferring such hateful titles as those given to children whose parents weren't married at the time of their conception. The four of them shuffled awkwardly around Emma's bed, unsure where to position themselves without touching someone else.

"I've summoned the doctor, and he should be here shortly," Marilyn said as she cleared the bedside tray to park her purse, her massive Bible, and her drink. "I'm sure he'll tell us what we can already see. This won't last long." Marilyn's prognosis went mostly unheard, which irritated her even further.

Judy stood on the other side of the bed from her brother, avoiding eye contact with everyone in the room who was conscious.

Do I know you? Judy asked in silence as she looked at the frail body lying between them. She had lived in a state of self-imposed exile from her family since 1976. That was the year her husband had come out of the closet and left for San Francisco with his lover, never to be heard from again. It was also the year her father had died.

Judy knew that Marilyn considered her to be the catalyst for both incidents. She never missed an opportunity to remind Judy how her very existence—not to mention the existence of that… that *daughter*—was a source of unending grief for poor Emma and would eventually kill her as surely as Judy's sin had caused her father to die of a broken heart. Judy had always craved her daddy's love, and as much as she hated Marilyn, she heard truth in her barbs. So for the past twenty-five years, Judy had simply checked out, determined to avoid the family who knew her past and her pain.

"When you coming to see me, hon?" her mother would ask when she called. Emma had consistently tried to pull her back, but just being in her mother's sweet presence rekindled Judy's emotional pain. "I'm just busy, Mom. Soon."

Judy assumed Stu and Marilyn were with Emma on the traditional family holidays. She saw her mother infrequently—on her own terms—and then only enough to assuage a little of the perennial guilt that was their family legacy.

Emma did manage to keep in touch with her granddaughter, Ashley. Emma hadn't driven in years, and Judy would not take Ashley to visit often, but the two talked by phone several times a week.

"How's my girl?" every call would begin. Judy would listen as Ashley recounted their conversations, quietly thankful that Emma had a full life of health and joy, busy caring for friends and neighbors around her little white home with the big front porch.

Ashley was shy and easily intimidated. Now in this hospital room, between her aunt's overwhelming presence and her dying grandmother, she could not bear to participate. The tiny ear buds of her portable CD player went undetected, allowing her to escape in her music. *God?* she prayed. *I don't even know who You are, but Grandma does. Don't let her die.*

So there they were, this little family of strangers, each isolated in his or her own thoughts, all introverts except for Marilyn, gathered to watch Emma die.

The summons to the hospital had come just before Marilyn's daily Bible reading. Not wanting to miss an opportunity to give a testimony of her faithfulness, she opened her King James Bible to the day's passage and began to read—aloud. "I'm sure you won't mind if I read from God's Word. 'Concerning Damascus. Hamath is confounded, and Arpad: for they have heard evil tidings: they are fainthearted…'"

No words of comfort or hope from the Gospels. Marilyn seemed unaware of the words she read. She trumpeted—as proof of her piety—the fact that she had read the Bible "cover to cover" every year for the past twenty years. "Gotta hide that word in your heart," she was fond of saying. Those who knew her were fond of saying behind her back, "Wish she'd pay attention to the parts about being nice."

Marilyn's Bible reading grew louder and more pointed. She was itching for a reaction. Judy finally gave her one.

"Will you shut up, Marilyn? Mom doesn't need this, and neither do we." Stu stared at his big sister, the hair on his neck standing up from the electricity of the storm that was about to break forth. Marilyn paused, looked at Judy with her patented pity-wrapped-in-righteousness look, then continued reading at an only slightly quieter volume, ignoring the rudeness of her sister-in-law-the-infidel.

Judy was more than a little surprised herself for telling the queen of bossiness what to do. She reached down to brush imaginary wisps of hair back across her mother's forehead. *Just let it go,* she told herself. But that's not what happened. She tried to keep quiet, but she lost it.

What Judy actually said to her sister-in-law was so venomous that the nurses heard and came in to break it up. As Marilyn continued reading the obscure passage from Jeremiah at the top of her lungs; as Ashley sat in the corner, her eyes closed, hugging her knees to her chest and listening to her music; as Stu tried to get between Judy and Marilyn before physical violence erupted; as Judy began screaming at him to get out of the way before she slapped him, too; as the entire team of nurses ran in to restore order, it was right then that Emma fluttered her eyes, surveyed the situation with great clarity and sadness, said her piece, then died.

Out in the hallway, a crowd of the people who loved Emma most had gathered, forbidden to enter the ICU room because they were not family.

A covey of Emma's peers were clustered in a corner, hands joined in prayer. "Lord, we just know that You still have plans for Emma. Restore her to health, Lord, we pray in Jesus' name." Widows all, with children and grandchildren spread throughout the country, they depended on one another for companionship, a helping hand, and of course their weekly Bunko game. Though no one would have ever said it aloud for fear of hurting the others, each one of these white-headed ladies was convinced she was Emma's very best friend. They weren't about to let such a friend leave for heaven if they could help it.

"Charmaine?" yelled Kamisha Whitlock. "You get down from there right now. Rudy? Get yourself over here before I swat you. Do you hear me? Jameel? Leave that man alone. I'm not foolin' with you now!"

There were at least a half-dozen noisy kids of all colors between the ages of six and ten running around the waiting room, too full of energy to grieve for more than moments at a time. They were latchkey kids who had jumped in the car with Emma's neighbors to the north—Kamisha and her son, Jameel—when word got out they were headed for the hospital. Every one of them clamored to go see "Miz Emma," because they'd all spent time after school in her kitchen, chewing brownies and slurping milk, while she planted seeds of hope in their fertile young minds.

The Korean grocer from the corner store, Mr. Kim, pretended to watch television. No one could see that his heart was breaking. The highlight of his week was a visit from Mrs. Estes. He believed that no one cared as much about him as she did. He might have been right.

In his loneliness he briefly considered her attention to be a prelude to romance but was dissuaded from this view by his daughter, who knew Emma's kindness extended to almost everyone.

"How are the citizenship classes going?" Emma would inevitably ask.

"Good," he would say, smiling and nodding.

"I'm so glad to hear it. This country needs more citizens with your diligence and character."

The thought that Emma might not be present when he received his American citizenship was too much to bear.

Hanging by the door—trying to look cool instead of concerned—was Clarence, who preferred to be called Chill-C. Clarence was a would-be rapper, whom Emma was tutoring through ninth-grade English lit. Behind the occasional crudeness of his rhyme, Emma saw a real creative streak, and she had been introducing him to Emily Dickinson and Robert Frost. Right now his mind was churning a rhyme: *Death so bad when they no one 'round you / Sometime you go befo' yo' work be through.*

Lindsey Carson was there with her six-month-old son, Brennan, and her dad, Tom. When Lindsey had found out in the eleventh grade that she was pregnant, the first person she told was Emma Estes. "I'm in trouble," she'd said before bursting into tears. Before even hearing what sort of trouble, Emma had embraced her with unconditional love and support.

"Mrs. E" had gone with her to talk to her parents. As predicted, her father had grown red faced, screamed, and told her to get out of his house. Mrs. E—all 110 pounds of her—had stood right up to Tom and said, "If that's how you really feel, I'll be glad to take her home with me." Then she had given him the one-minute version of the parable of the prodigal son, without sounding preachy at all. Lindsey's dad had cracked, had begun sobbing, and had practically run across the room to give his daughter the first real hug he'd given her in a decade.

Others were there as well, all drawn by a deep love for the woman who had held their neighborhood together like a hen keeping watch over her chicks. As they waited, all were remembering and then sharing one incident after another of how Emma Estes had invested in them, believed in them, and just simply loved them.

When the fight broke out, loud enough to be heard through the heavy doors of the ICU, the crowd listened with confusion. "What in the Sam Hill you reckon is going on in there?" Skeeter asked no one in particular. Since Emma's children were virtual strangers to the neighborhood, no one recognized them when they left abruptly. First Marilyn with Stu in tow, then a few minutes later Judy and Ashley. Thinking that perhaps these people had been here to see someone else, the crowd sat for another thirty minutes hoping and praying for Emma.

Finally Skeeter Wilson went to the nurses' station and inquired. While she was there, Barry Lamb, Marilyn's pastor, arrived at the waiting room. No one there seemed to know who Marilyn was; no one knew where she was. Skeeter came back to the waiting room—the unwilling bearer of bad news—just as Reverend Lamb walked to the nurses' station himself. When she told them Emma was gone, the grief came in waves, like hurricane rains. Unlike the family, who had been too angry at one another to process the reality of their mother's death, these people felt it to the marrow of their bones. The sobbing lasted for a long time.

"Did she say anything before she passed?" someone finally asked quietly.

"I don't know. The nurse didn't say," replied Skeeter.

It was a real shame that the waiting room crowd couldn't have been around her bed when it came time for Emma to go home. Every single one of them would have understood exactly what Emma had whispered with her last breath.

"Read the journal."

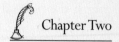

Chapter Two

Lord, I confess that I'm lazy. Today is one of those days when I would rather sit home and stare at the television all day. But I know You didn't create me to be a lump on this old couch, so I choose to get up and get out. I believe You have people for me to touch today, so I'll be paying attention for You to point them out to me.

Spiritual goal: To memorize the book of Philippians in the next year. That's only about two verses a week. If I don't keep stretching this old mind, it will only grow feeble and weak. I need all the oomph I can get out of it, Lord, so keep me sharp.

—from Emma's journal, June 23, 1990

The family met the next morning, another hot and steamy August day, to make arrangements. In the car on the way over to the funeral home, Marilyn had been priming her husband on what to say. "Now, Stuart, dear. We want to have your mother's funeral at our church on Friday. Not Thursday; that won't work for me."

"Why not have it at Mom's church?" asked Stu.

"Think about it, dear." She paused to sip her drink. "Your mother's friends are all dead. I doubt there will be five people there besides family if we have it at her church. We'll have it at our church so it's convenient for our friends. Besides, I know Pastor Lamb will preach the truth at the service, and the Lord knows that sister of yours and her illegitimate daughter need to get right with God."

Stu considered a number of responses to Marilyn's logic, but he was already fatigued by the whole ordeal, so he gave his standard reply. "Whatever you say, Marilyn. Whatever you say."

They entered the old funeral home on Antioch Road and were immediately greeted by a nondescript middle-aged man in a nondescript gray suit with an overly warm handshake.

"I'm so sorry to hear of your loss," he said.

Stu thought that the funeral business was a strange one indeed. *You say you are sorry for our loss, when in fact it's our losses that keep you in business.*

"Your sister and your mother's pastor are already here. Let me show you where they are waiting."

Marilyn stiffened upon hearing of Emma's pastor. This could complicate things.

Last night Marilyn had talked to the Reverend Barry Lamb for more than an hour after Stu had gone to bed. Lamb's wife suffered from debilitating depression, and Marilyn had managed to insert herself into the role of confidante that should have belonged to his wife. In addition to letting him vent about the struggles of ministry, Marilyn would stroke his ego and remind him just how valuable he was to their declining congregation.

The benefit to her was twofold. First, she was able to keep tabs on everyone and their various problems. Second, she maintained control over the weak-willed pastor. Since April, Marilyn had convinced him to finish his sermon manuscripts by Thursday so she could review them and make needed changes before Sunday. People were wondering why the usually meek pastor had been increasingly harsh and condemning in the pulpit in recent months.

"Have you made up your mind yet?" she had asked.

"You know it's not that simple," Lamb replied.

"There's a window of opportunity here, dear. We must grab it."

There was a long pause. "I can't do this."

"Don't tell me what you can or can't do, Barry. The truth is, you need me. Now let's get this funeral behind us and get on with our plan."

When Marilyn and Stu entered the room, Judy and Ashley were already seated at the table, as was a man in his early thirties. "Hi," he said, standing and smiling warmly. "I'm Toby Barnes, Emma's pastor."

"Why, look at you, dear," Marilyn crooned as she took his hand. "How sweet! A young man who wants to be a pastor when he grows up." Her tone grew sharper. "Don't tell me someone entrusted a pulpit to some, some *youth pastor*."

"Thanks for the compliment," Toby responded, refusing to be put off by Marilyn's inadequately disguised aggression. "I've been the pastor at Graystone Chapel for almost five years now. I came here right after I completed my master of divinity degree at the seminary over on North Oak Trafficway."

Before Marilyn could grill him further about his credentials and his theological correctness, the bland man in the bland suit interrupted. "Mr. and Mrs. Estes, please have a seat, and we'll get started. Pastor?"

Before Marilyn could object, Toby jumped in. "Let me start by saying that knowing your mother was one of my great joys in ministry. I've known few people who really exemplified the character of Jesus like your mother. She shared something of the difficult background your family has experienced…"

Judy stiffened at Toby's implication, wondering exactly what he knew of their family secrets. Had Emma ever mentioned her to this young man? Judy dealt with the residual fear and pain of her abusive father by pretending nothing had ever happened. If this pastor mentioned it aloud, she wasn't sure what might result.

"…and I can't tell you what an encouragement Emma has been to me personally."

"If so, then why weren't you at the hospital last night?" challenged Marilyn. No sooner had she said it than it dawned on her that Reverend Lamb had not arrived before they had left. She made a mental note to call and chastise him.

"Normally I would have come immediately," said Toby. "Yesterday afternoon one of our members lost his job unexpectedly and was very distraught, to the point that I was worried for his safety. I was with him for several hours and didn't get the message about your mother until after I left his home. By the time I got to the hospital, Emma was gone and your family had already left. There was quite a crowd gathered, as you know. Your mom had more friends than anyone I've ever met."

"We didn't see a soul there," sniffed Marilyn, not willing to let him off the hook.

"Please forgive me for not being there. I would have loved to have said good-bye to Emma before she went to be with Jesus. And by the way, your pastor, Reverend Lamb, was there as well. Nice man. Seemed a bit confused though. He said you had asked him to come, then you weren't there."

Stu was barely paying attention, waiting for the opportunity to speak as Marilyn had instructed. Sensing a pause in the conversation, he blurted out, "Uh, we were thinking, maybe, that we should have the funeral at our church."

Toby responded with another warm smile. "Stu, I'm here to serve your family in whatever way I can. But you should know that I have here a letter written by your mother with specific instructions about her funeral. Would you like me to read it to you?"

Stu looked at Marilyn for the answer. Her pursed lips let him know no answer was necessary.

Judy chimed in for the first time that morning. "Let's hear it."

The letter was dated almost six months earlier. It read:

Dear Pastor:

Thank you for taking time to visit with me last Thursday about the delicate matter of my own funeral. I know most people don't care to talk about such things, but honestly, I have no fear of death. Though I've been blessed with good health, I know that my Lord could call me home at any time. I have no desire to leave my friends and family, but I find that I spend quite a bit of time these days contemplating heaven. While I don't pretend to know exactly what it will be like, knowing I'll be in the presence of Jesus for all eternity is enough for me.

When the time comes to mark my passing from this life to one far better, I want you to lead the service. Of course, I want it held in Graystone Chapel, where our friends can gather to comfort one another and to hear you remind them of where I've gone. I trust you to bring a message that will not only help the ones I love grieve, especially my children, but also will encourage people to live their lives purposefully so they, too, can one day go home without regrets.

The letter went on to list several of Emma's favorite songs she wanted those congregated to sing, as well as the men she wanted to be pallbearers. Marilyn jumped in. "But I don't know a single one of these men," she objected. "Some of those names don't even sound American." Realizing how she sounded, she began to back up. "But, of course, you could make them honorary pallbearers, and we could get the deacons from *our* church to come."

"I think we should do whatever Mom wanted," said Judy, looking to her brother for confirmation.

"Yeah," Stu muttered, in spite of the sharp fingernails digging into his arm.

"There's more here," Toby said. "I've got a photocopy of this letter for each of you. She's got instructions about the dress she wanted to wear and a few things like that."

The funeral director spoke up. "Also, your mother has prepaid for her arrangements with us, and since she will be interred next to your father, that's taken care of as well. Of course, if you'd care to upgrade, I'd be happy to show you some options."

Stu wondered again at the director's choice of words. *Upgrade. Sounds like we're buying a car, not burying Mom.* No one responded to the director's offer, which fortunately he did not pursue.

Toby then asked about the date. "We can do this as early as tomorrow. Do you have more family coming from out of town?"

Marilyn was ready for at least one thing to go her way. "Friday. We want it on Friday." Everyone else seemed agreeable.

"Friday it is then. I know the ladies will want to have a meal for you at the church afterward; it's kind of our tradition. Anyone have any questions?"

Ashley, who up to this point had faded into the beige chair she sat on, raised her hand as if she were in school. Toby gave her a smile and nodded for her to speak.

"What did Grandma mean in her letter about going home?"

Before Toby could speak, Marilyn did. "You'll have to forgive the child, Pastor. She's obviously not been raised in a Christian environment."

Judy glared at Marilyn and tried to explain. "I haven't had much use for organized religion. Since my dad died—"

"Since you put a stake in his heart," Marilyn hissed.

Stu butted in. "Now, Marilyn, you need to quit picking on Judy." When he realized he had actually spoken aloud, he panicked. Contradicting his wife was something he did only rarely, accidentally, and never in public—because the consequences were so severe. But since she was momentarily stunned, he pressed on. "Judy had nothing to do with Dad's death. He smoked himself to death, pure and simple. She has a right to raise her daughter the way she wants to. I don't care to hear any more mean talk to Judy or anyone else. Let's try to be a family for once."

Marilyn glared at Stu, sputtered, started to speak, then stopped. With lips pursed tightly, she gathered herself and her things and made a dramatic exit from the room, slamming the door behind her. It was the best of all likely scenarios. Judy looked at her brother with newfound admiration.

Toby turned to Ashley, who had shrunk into her chair even further during the hostilities. "That's a great question, Ashley. When your grandmother spoke of going home, she was talking about heaven, because that's where her heart had been focused for years."

Ashley considered this answer, then replied quietly, "I'm glad she went there with no regrets."

"So am I, Ashley. So am I. Well, I think that's all we need to cover right now. I'll go and let you guys talk. Here's my number. Call me if you think of anything between now and Friday. I'll be in touch."

Disoriented at being alone with her brother without Marilyn, Judy didn't quite know what to say.

Stu finally broke the silence. "I'm sorry about what she said. She shoots off her mouth without thinking sometimes."

Judy couldn't help but smile. "Thanks for sticking up for me. I was afraid she was going to kill you for doing it though."

"I should have said something before. But you have to pick your battles with Marilyn."

Nodding in agreement, Judy gave small talk a shot. "So. How are you doing?" Noting his struggle for a reply, she clarified. "With all this."

Stu thought even longer before answering. "Not too good. I feel like such a lousy son. I should have spent more time with her. It's a crime to live so close to your mother and not even know who her friends are."

"I know how you feel. Mom would call every week. I'd make about two minutes of small talk, then hand the phone to Ashley."

"Why was it hard for you to talk with Grandma?" Ashley asked. "I think she's the easiest person in the world to talk to."

"A lot went on before you were born, honey," Judy said. "I have…had a way of making your grandmother unhappy, so to keep that from happening, I just stayed away."

"Mom always asked about you," Stu offered. "I didn't tell her we never talked. I just told her you were doing fine." He thought a minute and then asked, "You have been, haven't you?"

Judy paused before answering, wondering if he really expected an answer. She didn't think he even knew where she worked, so there was no use telling him she'd been passed over—again—for a promotion at the post office. According to Marilyn, their kids were perfect, so there was no point in telling him about the trials and tribulations of being a single mother trying to raise a daughter on the cusp of adolescence. Did he want to know about how much she struggled with her weight? Did he want to hear that she was already depressed at the thought of having to shop for a dress to wear to the funeral? She definitely knew he didn't want to hear about her loneliness, her frequent bouts of discouragement, and the early onset of menopause.

"Sure, we've been fine. Haven't we, Ash?"

The funeral home director came back in and gave them some paperwork to sign. As they walked to the parking lot together, Stu put an arm awkwardly around his sister's shoulders. "I'm sorry I haven't been a better brother," he mumbled. "I'll try to do better."

"And I'm sorry about freaking out at the hospital yesterday," Judy offered.

"Would you be willing to go by Mom's house and get her dress and the other stuff they wanted?" Stu asked, handing her a key.

"Don't you think Marilyn will want to do it?"

"Marilyn's done about enough for one day. Don't worry about her." He paused. "She's never hit me yet."

But when he glanced up and saw Marilyn at the wheel of her car, a dark green Jaguar, the look she gave him made him drop his arm from Judy's shoulders and shove his hands in his pockets. Turning his head so Marilyn couldn't read his lips, he said, "I swear she's got powers like Superman. She knows I was talking about her. Guess I'll be on bread and water for a few weeks. But that's all right."

"Thanks. For everything." Judy turned toward her own ten-year-old Jeep Cherokee. "I'll go by the house and pick up that dress. Later we can get together and go through her stuff and decide…" She couldn't finish.

"Yeah, we'll get together."

As Judy drove to the house at 411 Longfellow Street, she was shocked to see how much the neighborhood had changed since she had grown up there. *Surely it hasn't been that long since I've been to the house,* she thought but was at a loss to remember the last time she and Ashley had made this trip. After pulling into the driveway, Judy killed the engine and sat there just looking.

"It looks a lot smaller than it used to."

"So did you have to walk ten miles to school in the snow?" teased Ashley.

"Uphill. That way," she said and pointed. "Come on. I'll need your help."

"To pick up a dress?"

"To fight off the ghosts of years past."

Inside the door they were immediately engulfed in hot air scented with lavender and a whiff of mothballs. *Smells just like Mom,* Judy thought. She was surprised by the emotion that came with the scent. She tried to fight that first tear, knowing if it came, she'd never hold back the flood. She lost.

As she collapsed on the old but spotless sofa, her tears gave way to choking sobs. Unsure what else to do, Ashley sat beside her. The girl had seen her mother depressed, even seething with rage, but had rarely seen her cry.

After several minutes Judy collected herself. Embarrassed by her reaction, she attempted an explanation, mostly to herself. "I can't believe how it hit me all at once. After years of trying to wall myself off from Mom, I walk in the door and wham." With that, she began to cry again, although not as hard this time. "Promise me you'll never walk away from me the way I walked away from my mom."

Not knowing how to answer, Ashley held her mother, then began to cry herself.

Eventually the two gathered their composure and began walking through the small Craftsman-style bungalow. "I'd turn on the air conditioner, but we won't be here long enough for it to cool down."

"Wow. Grandma sure kept a clean house," Ashley offered, surveying a curio cabinet filled with intricate glass figurines, all without a speck of dust.

"I could keep a clean house too if that was my full-time job. You could pitch in once in a while, you know." Judy's uncharacteristic softness had retreated.

"I was just, like, making a comment. No need to take it so personal."

As they entered Emma's bedroom, Judy went to the closet while Ashley sat on the bed and began to look at the things on the nightstand. Just outside the window, blooming double hollyhocks stood at attention despite the heat.

"Was this my grandfather?" she asked, holding up a picture.

Leaving her task, Judy sat down beside her daughter. "Yep." The picture was hard to look at; the memories of her father, Frank

Estes, were too shrouded in pain. Nonetheless, she swallowed her resistance and made herself look at it, surprised that Ashley didn't remember ever having seen his photograph.

"That's him. Look at those ears. Kinda shaped like yours, aren't they?"

Ashley resumed her browsing. She picked up a Bible and a leather-bound journal. "Look at how worn this Bible is. I wish we'd known. We could have gotten her a new one for her birthday or something."

Judy paused from deciding which blue dress her mother was talking about and, from the back of the closet, looked over her shoulder. "Huh. I guess when you get old, reading the Bible is a good thing to do. You know, like studying for finals."

Ashley missed the point of her mother's lame joke. "Have you ever read the Bible, Mom?"

"No, I haven't. We didn't go to church much when I was little. Grandma got interested in religion after your Granddad died. I guess she found comfort in it."

"How come we don't go to church? Couldn't we use some comfort too?"

"What church? Your Aunt Marilyn's? What kind of church would want someone like me in it?"

"What do you mean? You're just like anyone else."

"Never mind. I just meant I'm not the churchgoing type, that's all. What do you think about this dress? I can't tell which one she wanted, but this one looks newer and in a little better shape. I wish she would have let us buy her something new."

"Toby seems nice." Ashley flipped through the old Bible, noticing that many pages had verses underlined and notes scribbled in the margins. "Do you think I could have this Bible to remember her by?"

"Take it. I'm sure Marilyn has stacks of Bibles at her house."

Ashley then started flipping through the journal. The first entry was dated August 24, 1976. "Wow, look at this. Grandma started keeping a journal over twenty-five years ago."

Before Judy could respond, the doorbell rang, and she went to answer it. Six elderly women were on the porch, white hair glowing. "You must be Emma's daughter. I'm Skeeter Wilson, and we're Emma's friends," said the leader of the pack. She introduced each by name while Judy absent-mindedly held the dress.

"I see you found the right one," Skeeter offered. "Emma had us all over for tea one day and modeled three different dresses for us. She'd lie down on the couch and fold her hands across her chest so we could see how she'd look in her casket." The women started to giggle at the memory, but their humor faded in a hurry when they remembered she was really gone and they saw the look on Judy's face.

"Please forgive us," Skeeter begged. "We meant no disrespect. It's just that your mother was such a card. Who else could do something so morbid and make it funny? She kept everyone around her in stitches most of the time."

Judy searched for a childhood memory of her mother being a card and found none. She hesitated to invite the women in. "It's awfully hot in here. We were just leaving."

"We can't stay either," Skeeter said, as she led her geriatric gang into the living room. "We just saw you over here and wondered if you needed anything."

"Thanks, but no, I think we're set. Ashley and I were about done." Hearing her name, Ashley walked into the room. Skeeter stood up and gave the girl such a hug that she dropped the Bible and journal. Judy picked them up and placed them on the table, then laid the dress on top of them.

"Well, look at you, princess. You are just as beautiful as your grandmother said." Ashley blushed, unused to being the center of attention. "Honey, I need you to help me. I've got a big platter of food in the fridge for you to take home, but I'm too old and frail to carry it. Come on."

Accustomed to being told what to do, Ashley followed the woman across the street. She returned a few minutes later loaded down with enough fried chicken, potato salad, and carrot cake to feed the U.S. Olympic team. She and her mother were several miles down the road before Ashley shrieked, "My stuff! Did you pick up Grandma's Bible and journal for me?"

"Relax. It's in the backseat."

Ashley dove over the seat and emerged seconds later with the Bible. "You didn't get the journal. We've got to go back."

"Honey, we don't have time to go back. I've got to make some phone calls and run a few errands. We'll go by the house after the funeral, and you can get it then. We'll have plenty of time to look through her things and pick out some other mementos to remember her by."

Chapter Three

Money is not growing on the trees in this yard, and Frank didn't leave much behind. I'm too old to get a job. So I had better learn something about budgeting. If I can't make more, I'm going to learn to spend less.

Intellectual goal: To start keeping and living by a budget. Every day I'll record every penny I spend. At the end of every month, I'll be able to see where I spent those pennies and decide if that's how I want to spend them.

—FROM EMMA'S JOURNAL, JANUARY 1, 1978

Ben Shoffner climbed down from the cab of the old International truck and walked around to the dock stairs. The faded bandanna wrapped around his head was soaked in sweat. The bandanna covered his balding top; below, a graying, braided ponytail lay damp on his back. As he crossed the parking lot, Rita Vallejos, the manager and founder of Helping Hands Ministries, walked toward him in the heat, eager to greet her new driver back from his first run.

"So how'd it go for you?" Rita asked.

"Pretty good, I guess. I only got lost once. That was in one of those rich neighborhoods I've never been in before."

"Let's look at your load of treasure, shall we?" They returned to the old International, and Ben swung open the clasp and raised the back door of the panel truck on its tracks. Inside were mostly trash bags of clothes no one wanted anymore and a few pieces of broken-down furniture.

"I hate to say it, but it looks like junk to me," Ben offered.

Rita smiled. "It's true that most people don't give away things until they're done with them. But there are exceptions. In those more affluent neighborhoods you were talking about, some ladies give away their entire wardrobe once a year to make room for all the new clothing they've binged on. Sometimes we get clothes in here with the tags still on them."

"Here's a bag of old board games."

"Let me have that one. Sometimes old toys and games become collectibles that are worth some real money. Which reminds me, Ben. Make sure you remember our rules. You may not keep anything that you pick up for your personal use. If you see something you could use at home, then just let me know, and I'll let you have it for the price it would sell for in the thrift shop."

Ben studied her face, wondering why she had brought this up again.

"I'm sorry," she said, touching his forearm. "I didn't mean to imply that you'd do anything dishonest. It's just that we've had other drivers who would dig through their collections before coming back here and sell the real antiques to supplement their salary. One young driver found a metal lunchbox from the sixties and sold it to a collectible store for a hundred dollars."

Not knowing how to respond, Ben changed the subject. "So what happens to this junk now?"

Rita relished every opportunity to talk about this ministry that she, along with the support of local churches, had founded. "The thrift store is one way for us to generate a little income to help with our other ministries. The volunteers sort everything out. The clothes that are too worn to wear will be sold for recycling. Anything that's wearable gets cleaned and put on a rounder inside the shop. The furniture and other items go on sale as well. Then the proceeds from the thrift store go to help us take care of other needs. If donations to the food pantry get low, sometimes we have to buy groceries to supplement—staples like peanut butter and canned tuna. Seems we never run out of canned green beans though. Another service we provide is assistance with people's utilities, once they've been screened. You know, to make sure they aren't running a con game or something."

Ben wondered how desperate a man would have to be to turn to such an organization for help. He'd seen some pretty lean times, but he couldn't imagine swallowing enough pride to ask for groceries. He looked up from his thoughts to see Rita watching him.

"So that's it for me?"

"That's it. Good first day. We'll see you tomorrow."

His old turquoise Chevy Apache pickup had what Ben called "two-fifty air conditioning": two windows rolled down at fifty miles per hour. Driving home, he felt a growing urge to stop at one of the numerous liquor stores that lined the highway. *Nothing like a cold beer at the end of a long, hot day,* he rationalized. Knowing he hadn't stopped at one beer since the first time he had tasted it in high school, he kept driving and reached for his water jug instead. The ice had long since melted, and the lukewarm water only strengthened his urge for a brew.

Determined to fight the craving, he turned his thoughts toward home. Sunshine would be home by now. School had started this week, and Sunny had been counting the days. The twelve-year-old, actually almost thirteen-year-old, was—in her father's terms—"a brainiac." The counselor at school referred to her as "exceptionally gifted." Ben just shook his head, clueless about the source of her academic ability. Her test scores placed her in advanced classes.

This year Sunny was taking high-school honors algebra in the seventh grade. "I can't even spell algebra," her dad told her upon hearing the news, proud of her while shamed by his own low-achieving life. He repeated a line he'd told her a thousand times: "Maybe you can go to college and make something of yourself."

Ben thought how Sunny had looked this morning, all dressed up for school. Her long blond hair hung free. She looked much like her mother had the first time Ben saw her.

All day long Ben had been savoring the memory of his wife. Linda had been a beautiful woman, full of life and creativity. Ben met her at an art show. He was displaying his sculpture. She had both her pottery and her watercolors showing there. Before the show was over, they were a couple. They married six months later in a field of wildflowers at the vernal equinox. At the time, all their friends had described it as "groovy."

Linda's father had been a loud, verbally abusive man. She had grown up under the punishment of his tongue, watching her mother grow smaller as the years went by. Her parents were both dead now, and in her Big Ben she found the gentleness, sweetness, and patience she'd never known in a man. "Because of you, my past has ceased to influence my present or my future," she had told him on their wedding day as she spoke the vows she had written.

Ben had the heart and soul of an artist and saw in this relationship a chance to create a masterpiece. He gave the same considerable attention to nurturing their love that he had given to his massive abstract sculptures.

Though they took no precautions to prevent them, children were not a part of their early life together. Neither made much money from their art, but they enjoyed the freedom that was theirs. Living a simple life, Ben and Linda had joy.

One dreary winter day Ben had come in from the garage of their little rented house—what he called his "studio"—to find Linda in tears. "What is it?" he asked, surprised by the departure from her upbeat self. Holding up a plastic strip with a streak of blue, she sobbed. Not recognizing what it was, Ben attempted a guess. "Do you have a fever?"

Linda laughed. "No, you goof. It's a pregnancy test. I'm pregnant. *We're* pregnant. We're gonna have a baby!"

And that's how, at the age of forty, an aging hippie sculptor became a father. As they sat on the couch that afternoon, the clouds parted for a few moments, and the rays of the setting sun came through the kitchen window. "Sunshine. That's what we'll name her," he said when he could finally speak without blubbering.

Ben's thoughts drifted back to the present. A small neon sign in the window of a local pub caught his attention: Cold Beer, Cold A/C. He gripped the warm steering wheel still harder and pressed on.

Sunny had been two when Ben found Linda crying again. Thinking it was news of another baby, he plopped down expectantly. But this time it was a lump in Linda's breast. A year later she was gone, leaving Ben alone with a preschooler to raise.

Losing Linda had been the beginning of Ben's painful downhill slide. He was unable to create art in his grief, and truth be told, Linda's work had always had more commercial appeal, making her the primary breadwinner. Ben had virtually no marketable skills. A neighbor had told him about Headstart, so he had enrolled Sunny in preschool at the age of three and had begun a seemingly endless string of bottom-of-the-food-chain jobs.

That's when the heavy drinking had started. He would drop in at the bar down the street after work. One night he forgot to go home.

Ben had lost custody of Sunny for almost a year because of that incident. When he finally got her back after agreeing to enter a support group, he was scared straight for almost six years. But then he reverted to his old pattern of buying first a six-pack and then a twelve-pack and drinking alone after Sunny went to bed. Not only did this new habit keep him from repeating the sin of his past, it kept him from driving drunk. His driver's license had become his passport to work as a local truck driver. But far too many nights Ben would pass out on the couch, awakening to find his little girl placing the empty cans—"dead soldiers," he called them—in the trash and starting the coffee.

Pulling into the driveway of his rented home, he saw Sunny through the picture window. "Hi, Dad," she said when he walked in, her disposition just like her name. "So how'd the new job go?"

"Not bad. Not too hard. Just drive around to the houses of people who want to get rid of their junk. Saw some rich people's houses today over by the airport, near Tiffany Springs. You keep doing well in school, maybe you'll live in a big house over there someday."

"If I do, you'll be living with me. What do you want to do for supper?"

"It's too hot to eat right now. Let's go out on the porch and hope for some breeze."

They sat together in the rusty old patio chairs left by the former tenant, Sunny telling him all about her new teachers. She'd started middle school the year before, so the routine of changing classes was familiar to her. She talked about her friends, old and new. After a while, Sunshine left to start her homework. Ben stayed behind, unbuttoning his shirt in search of a breeze. He needed a shower but couldn't get up from the lawn chair. The soft drink Sunny had handed him was better than the tepid water in his jug, but he craved something else. Still, he sat, waiting.

It was only much later, after a sandwich supper and after Sunny completed her homework and went to bed, that he drove two blocks to the convenience store and got the cold beverages he craved.

The next morning Ben felt guilty as usual and buried his dead soldiers in the trash before Sunny got up. He was relieved when Rita greeted him with the dispatch list. "Only one stop today. It's a house at 411 Longfellow in Claycomo. The woman who lived there died. Her daughter-in-law will meet you. She's donating everything in the house. I'll send Tim with you to help load."

Tim, who was "volunteering" as part of his probation, sat in silence all the way. That was fine with Ben, who wasn't feeling especially talkative himself. He suspected that Sunny knew what he'd done but hadn't mentioned it. Maybe it was his own shame or just her embarrassment, but either way he hated the way it made him feel.

When they got to the house, a beautiful Jaguar sat in the driveway. They knocked on the door, and a big woman opened it, drink in one hand, cell phone glued to her ear. She made them wait almost fifteen minutes while she finished the conversation, which, from what Ben could tell, consisted of her telling her husband what for. She was almost beautiful, regal like a queen, until you heard the tone of her voice. Ben felt sorry for her husband. No man deserved to be talked to like that.

When she got off the phone, she pointed to several boxes by the door. "One of you put those things in my trunk. And be careful; there's china in those two big ones. Then the rest of it goes on your truck. And hurry. The Realtor is coming by at four, and I want all this junk out of here by then."

Ben simply nodded, assessing quickly there was no way all this was going to fit in his truck. He told her, "We'll get the furniture first. You got any more boxes for the rest of it?"

"Do *I* have any boxes? Why didn't you think to bring any with you? That's your job! Good grief, what kind of stupid people do they hire down at that place?"

Biting his lip, Ben kept quiet and motioned for Tim to grab the other end of the sofa. His passive nature and need for a job kept him from saying what was on his mind, but his guts simmered in resentment.

The two men worked wordlessly as the big woman left occasionally but spent most of the morning supervising their every move. When they got back to Helping Hands around half past eleven to unload the morning's work, Tim walked off, never to be seen again. The manager found boxes and recruited three volunteers, who followed Ben in their car back to Longfellow Street.

Ben had intended to sit in the shade on the big porch and eat his lunch before starting in again, but the boss woman arrived and starting cracking the whip. The volunteers packed boxes; Ben rolled them to the truck on his two-wheeler.

As the afternoon wore on—hotter than ever with no chance of a summer shower to cool things down—Ben began to struggle. *I'm too old to be working this hard.* He paused briefly before pulling his load backward up the ramp of the truck, then began his ascent. His fatigue overcame him halfway up, and his sweaty hand lost its grip on the load. He fell backward, hitting his hip on the edge of the ramp before falling off on the driveway. The boxes fell forward, spilling their contents everywhere.

Ben sat up, aching but relieved to see no apparent damage. Before he could get to his feet, *she* appeared. "What happened out here, you clumsy fool? Look at this! You'd better hope that nothing is broken. If it is, I'll report you to your supervisor for carelessness." Before she could go on, her cell phone rang, saving Ben from additional abuse.

As he picked himself up, he heard her say on the phone, "Why, hello, Pastor. I was just helping one of the workers here retrieve some items he dropped. I wanted to talk to you about Mom's funeral. There's been a change in plans…"

Ben began reloading the boxes. Books and knickknacks mostly. A worn leather volume caught his attention. Later he would wonder why he even picked it up. He leafed through it, looking up occasionally to make sure she wasn't watching. Fortunately, she had headed back into the house to be near the air conditioner.

The book appeared to be a journal of some kind. It was filled with a woman's handwriting, that beautifully uniform Palmer script from back in the day when all women wrote like schoolteachers. He read the first paragraph, dated August 24, 1976.

Unwilling to live my life in the future the way I've lived it in the past, I resolve that—submitted to God and with His help—I will become each day more like the person He created me to be.

Ben looked around to make sure no one was watching. For reasons he didn't yet understand, he limped to the cab of the truck and stuck the old journal inside the faded red-and-white cooler that served as his lunchbox.

Chapter Four

I keep hearing about how computers are going to change our lives. I figure there's not much about this old lady's life that a computer could fix. But the man at the computer store says that before long they will be like telephones; everyone will have one, and we'll talk to each other on them. We'll even pay our bills over the computer. Imagine that. He told me about something called "e-mail." Seems that you can send a letter over the phone lines just by hitting a button. No stamp, no time delay, just boom—there it is. I don't know exactly who I'll send o mail to since no one I know has a computer, but I might as well get on board. Maybe it will help the neighborhood kids with their studies.

Intellectual goal: Buy a computer this month, and learn to use e-mail.

—FROM EMMA'S JOURNAL, SEPTEMBER 29, 1995

The night before the funeral a violent storm blew through, dropping an inch of rain in less than an hour and blowing branches off the trees. A small tornado touched down a few miles east of town, but the only damage was to a barn and an abandoned house.

During the storm Judy had awakened from a bad dream at three o'clock and had been unable to go back to sleep. The dream was a familiar one. She had experienced it in several versions for most of her life, ever since the event that had first triggered it. In her dream her father was yelling at her—his face flushed and eyes bright—asking questions she couldn't quite understand. She was about seven and hiding in the closet because she had heard him shouting and cursing at her mother. If only she could have understood what he wanted, she could have made him stop yelling at her. She was so frightened, and her tears made him scream all the more. Then she would awaken. And lie there crying, the memories as vivid as if they had happened the night before.

Finally getting up around half past five, she made coffee and tried not to think about what lay ahead that day. Her dream faded, but the reality of the funeral turned her thoughts to her mother.

When did things between Mom and me fall apart? As best she could remember, it began in her late teen years. Emma called Judy "boy crazy" and had objected when she began dating Chuck. "Something troubles me about him, but I can't put my finger on it," was all she would say.

If only she had listened. Her mother had learned some things about discerning trouble over the course of her own less than healthy marriage. Emma, Stu, and Judy had all learned the art of being invisible when Frank Estes was in one of his moods.

After Chuck and Judy decided to get married right out of high school, Emma put the lid on her concerns and did the best she could to accept Chuck into the family. Even Frank came around, sometimes taking Chuck fishing with him on Saturday mornings.

For four years she and Chuck lived together, poor but mostly happy. At least that's what she had thought. She got a decent job at the downtown post office while Chuck attended Rockhurst College, working toward a career in advertising. Chuck stayed out late a lot of nights; he told her he was at the library studying.

When Judy found out the truth about what he was doing those evenings, her shame almost buried her. Because her parents had eventually grown so fond of Chuck—they loved his sense of humor, his warmth, and his ability to turn ordinary pantry ingredients into works of art—she tried to withhold the truth, that he was moving to San Francisco with his boyfriend.

When her mother asked, "Is there someone else?" Judy just nodded, allowing her to fill in the blanks. Her father hounded her for details, and when he eventually found out what had happened, his reaction highlighted both his cruel streak and his misogyny. "What woman would be such a disappointment to her husband that he would leave her for a man? I swear, Judy. You mess up everything, don't you?"

Time did not heal anything. The longer Judy dwelt on the loss in her life, the worse her free fall. When her father died of a heart attack just three months later, Judy crashed. Her strategy for coping with her double-barreled emotion in the months that followed consisted of withdrawing from everyone and everything she had once enjoyed, including her mother. At the core of her emotions was bitterness toward her mother. Sometimes she thought that if her mother had just tried to protect them better…even though she knew Emma had coped the only way she knew how.

Complicating matters was the addition of a sister-in-law to the family. Stu and Marilyn had been married less than a year when Chuck left and Frank died. Marilyn was a pious girl even then, insisting on Stu's conversion before she'd marry him. It was only the first of a lifelong series of projects to recreate Stu into…something. No one could ever figure out what it was she wanted him to become, including Stu.

After Chuck left, Marilyn had come to Judy's house and spent two and a half hours lecturing her about the sin of divorce and trying to get Judy to turn before she burned. "If you divorce Chuck, you will be out of God's will for the rest of your life. The Bible says God hates divorce, and that means He hates people who get divorced. If you care about your soul, then you'll stay in this marriage."

Judy's great relief was that Marilyn did not have all the details, or her sermons would have been even more vicious.

When daylight came, it was slightly cooler than the sultry August mornings that had preceded it. As the summer sun sent its growing warmth through her kitchen window, Judy stood to refill her coffee cup, wanting to change the channels of her mind. The cat meowed, ready to be fed. But when she sat back down, she mentally picked up where she had left off.

After her world had fallen apart with Chuck, she'd tried to pray, hoping that somehow God would make it all better. But her sister-in-law's strong-arm tactics had made her decide that if Marilyn was God's representative, she didn't need God after all.

It was after her dad's funeral that Judy's family ties had come completely unraveled. That day Marilyn had announced to everyone that Frank Estes's death was not only a by-product of Judy's divorce but also the consequence of Judy's refusal to become a Christian. "God will do whatever it takes to get your attention, mark my words. Until you repent, there'll be no rest for you. Ever."

That prophecy had been true enough. The next twelve years were foggy memories, ones she'd worked hard to put out of her mind. She'd had a job—a numbing, mindless job—but one that paid well enough. She'd had few friends, none who was close. Her insecurity about her appearance and her femininity would drive her to lose a dramatic amount of weight in a mission to become attractive enough, deserving enough. Always eventually failing, in her pain she would turn to the refrigerator, where she would find a solace, albeit temporary, that no man could give, and her weight would balloon again.

Every few years, during one of her "thin" periods, her loneliness would lead her to a certain type of man—the type who took advantage of her vulnerability. A few moved in for a short while, but those relationships never lasted more than a few weeks. When they moved out, the binging began again.

When she was almost thirty-seven, one of those relationships with a younger man named Tony resulted in Ashley's conception. She'd often thought if she'd given Tony half a chance, they might have made it. But she kicked him out the day after learning of her pregnancy, never seeing him again, never telling him about their daughter.

Over the years Judy had done her best to avoid the subject, but when pressed by Ashley, she'd invented a story about Tony that seemed to satisfy the girl. Another reason Judy tried to keep Ashley away from her family was that, so far, she'd never had to tell her about Chuck. Some things were better left in the past.

Her thoughts were interrupted by Ashley's arrival in the kitchen. Judy looked at her and was moved by the girl's innocent beauty. The two had their differences—Ashley's entrance into puberty was accompanied by the usual mother-daughter struggles—but this morning, before anything could break the mood, Judy's heart was tender toward Ashley.

"Good morning, sunshine. How'd you sleep?"

"Why'd you call me sunshine?" Ashley grumped. "That's the name of a girl in my algebra class."

"No reason. Just that your arrival brightened my morning." Ashley rolled her eyes, then walked over to the refrigerator to pour herself a glass of juice. The eye roll was usually guaranteed to yank Judy's chain. Not this morning. "What's this girl Sunshine like?" she pressed.

Never the morning person, Ashley leaned against the counter and chugged her orange juice before answering the question. "I haven't talked to her, but she seems nice. Quiet like me. I don't think she's got much money. Her clothes are, like, kind of old. But she's nice, and, like, really smart."

"So are you, Ash. You wouldn't be taking a high school algebra class if you weren't really smart yourself."

"You're my mom. It's your job to believe that."

Neither was in the mood for breakfast. Judy had put away most of a half-gallon of ice cream after Ashley had gone to bed. Her daughter was suddenly in the mood for conversation, an increasingly rare occurrence these days. "Tell me stories about Grandma."

Judy looked at the bottom of her empty coffee cup. "I wish I had more stories to tell. I don't think the mother I knew growing up is the same woman that died on Monday."

"What does that mean?"

"Something the pastor said the other day. That Mom had more friends than anyone else he knew. When I was growing up, Mom was quiet, not very sure of herself. She was always sweet but not very outgoing. Her whole life was about taking care of me and Stu."

"Maybe she had to, like, start over after you guys left and Grandpa died."

"I'm sure that's exactly what happened. I just wish I hadn't pulled away from her." With that statement of regret, Judy found herself telling her twelve-year-old daughter an age-appropriate but truthful version of the events she'd been reliving since before the dawn.

Stu and Marilyn lived in the Riverbend subdivision of Overland Park in a house too big for their needs, surrounded by neighbors they didn't know, from which they commuted to jobs they didn't like. Overland Park was in Johnson County, the most affluent county in both the state of Kansas and the metropolitan Kansas City area.

Their sons had attended the prestigious Pembroke Country Day School and now attended first-rank universities. Dale was at Stanford, Rick at Brown. Neither had bothered to come home for more than a few days at a time since leaving for his freshman year.

The center of Marilyn's universe was their small, dysfunctional church, where she ruled over everyone, including the pastor, the Rev. Barry Lamb. Stu attended with her, and had perfected the art of sleeping in church while appearing to be deep in thought.

Stu had spent most of the previous night on his ham radio, a hobby he had acquired mainly as a way of staying out of Marilyn's way. Like his sister, he, too, had been dealing with regrets of not being closer to his mother; he, too, bore the emotional scars of an abusive father.

About two in the morning, Stu had found himself sharing those regrets with a fellow ham operator in New Zealand. He'd gone to bed after that and had slept well until Marilyn had awakened him at seven for "morning devotions." The drill was this: Armed with a big glass of Diet Coke, she insisted that he sit quietly while she read her daily Bible selection aloud. As he almost always did when she was in the Old Testament prophets, he withdrew into his own thoughts. Embarrassed by his conversation the night before, he wondered why he'd told a stranger things that he'd never been able to say to anyone face to face.

"Then he put out the eyes of Zedekiah; and the king of Babylon bound him in chains…"

Stu checked out again, hoping they'd get to the New Testament soon, where at least he had a clue what was going on. Both their sons had finally returned the calls Marilyn had placed earlier in the week about their grandmother. In spite of their mother's insistence, both had chosen not to come home for her funeral.

"I don't want to sound cold, Dad, but it's not like we were really close or anything," the older son had told him. That part broke his heart; that was his fault. He should have taken the lead in making sure the boys knew their grandmother. He had set a bad example. He struggled to figure out why he had pulled so far away from his mother. She had an optimistic view of people—she was even nice to Marilyn in spite of how bossy and demanding she was. Now if his mother had been like his wife…

Stu was pretty sure that his boys would both move as far away from their mother as possible after college. Who could blame them? But he had no excuses. Emma had been a good mother. He was just a poor excuse for a son and a father, end of story.

Finally the drone of Marilyn's voice stopped, signaling it was his turn. He voiced the same prayer he prayed virtually every morning. He could say it in his sleep, but it placated Marilyn, so he didn't dare change it. After the amen came the real prayer, his silent secret prayer: *Dear God, please help me endure one more day with this woman.*

After she raised her head from prayer, Marilyn asked, "Stuart, are you all right?"

Taken aback, Stu became wary. "I'm fine. Why do you ask?"

"Just wondering. Your mother and all. Just wondering how you are coping."

Stu's mind ran a search, trying to remember when—if ever—she had expressed concern for anyone but herself. "I'm fine."

Stu headed out the door to get a cup of coffee and pick up his suit from the cleaners. Marilyn sat in the living room and pondered her life and her marriage. *He's pulling away.* She was sure of it. *He has every reason to,* she thought. *He must hate me.* She was aware of her dominance over him, but it seemed justified. *He's so mousy he needs someone to take charge for him.* But she had sensed a growing resentment for a while. For the first time, he had stood up to her. That frightened her.

As she headed upstairs to take her shower, Marilyn wondered if they had ever really loved each other. They had married after a very short courtship. She was on the rebound from a broken engagement, and Stuart Estes had never had a single date before. Once she set her sights on Stu, he never really knew what happened.

A girlfriend had asked her why. Why Stu? To this day she wasn't sure. He was not overly handsome. He was at the top of his class academically, and a summer internship assured him of a great job in Kansas City after graduation. Maybe that had been it. Getting away from Texas and her family had seemed so important back then. Now both her parents were dead, and she didn't even have a current address for her only brother.

Neither had ever talked much of love, or anything else for that matter. In the early days they were tied together by a clumsy passion. But after two sons in less than three years, those ties were loosed. They had little in common—no mutual friends, no mutual hobbies, no mutual goals. They coexisted, both playing their roles.

But things were about to change. No longer a naive college girl, now she had a chance to make a more deliberate choice.

Chapter Five

There's a nice new Korean man with a daughter who just moved
in four houses down. Someone told me he bought the little grocery
on Claycomo Boulevard. He has a daughter who's in high school.
Since he's a single man, I must be careful about appearances, so I'd
better not take food over. Don't want to give the girls something
to talk about! I'll invite them both to church and pray for them
daily.

Spiritual/Relational goal: To share the gospel of Jesus with this
man and his daughter within ninety days.

—FROM EMMA'S JOURNAL, FEBRUARY 28, 1992

The summer sun, amplified by the humidity, was already beat-
ing down when the family arrived at the church in the limousine provided by the funeral home. They were shocked by the
full parking lot, as it was still thirty minutes until the service.

"Who in the world are all these people?" wondered Marilyn
aloud. "I fully expected *our* congregation to be here for us, but I
don't recognize any of these cars." At that moment, a light blue
Buick pulled into the parking lot, and Marilyn went over to greet
her pastor. As Reverend Lamb got out of his car, Marilyn found
herself once again assessing the man. He was tall and slim, immaculately dressed, his gray mane swept back in waves. But there was

something weak about him. She could never decide if it was his chin or his eyes that hinted at a softness on the inside.

"So glad you are here, Pastor. I need you to lean on to make it through this hour."

"Wow, Toby was right," said Ashley. "Who would have thought that Grandma had so many friends?"

As the family walked in, Toby was there to greet them, looking decidedly uncomfortable in his one suit. Theirs was an informal congregation, and Toby only put on coat and tie for "marrying and burying." His straight brown hair was standing up in a rooster tail in the back, which only accentuated his boyish appearance.

After giving them time for a private viewing of Emma in a small room just off the sanctuary, Toby took them to his office, where he showed them the order of service Emma had requested. He asked Reverend Lamb if he would give the invocation, and before the man could answer, Marilyn wanted to know if Toby was going to preach a message with some real gospel in it since there would be plenty of sinners present. She said this while giving a not-so-subtle nod of her chin in Judy and Ashley's direction.

Toby assured her he had the message all worked out just as he and Emma had agreed. Before Marilyn could press him for details, there was a knock on the door.

In walked six people, four men and two women. Marilyn's mouth dropped. "These are the people that I mentioned to you at the funeral home," explained Toby. "Emma's friends and neighbors that she had asked to serve as pallbearers."

Marilyn stood and pirouetted on her tiny feet to face the Graystone pastor. Her face was the picture of shock and disbelief. "What is going on here?" she said in a mock whisper. "Women pallbearers? I can't believe what I'm seeing! What kind of church is this? Pastor, do you see what I'm seeing?" she asked, now looking at Barry Lamb.

Reverend Lamb looked as though he was searching for the words Marilyn wanted him to say. Toby started to speak, Marilyn started to spew, but Stu interrupted them both, finding his spine for the third time in a week. "These are Mom's friends. There's nothing evil here. I'm no theologian, but even I know there's nothing in the Bible that talks about pallbearers, much less who can be one. If they were friends of Mom, that's enough for me."

Judy and Ashley quickly voiced their agreement. Once again Toby started to speak and was cut off. "I cannot be a part of such blasphemy," Marilyn blustered. She managed to work up a tear of shame. "I shall be out in the parking lot with Reverend Lamb and the elders from our church, praying that God will intervene! Stuart, if you have any sense of respect for the Lord or your mother, you'll come with me."

In the silence that followed her departure—with Reverend Lamb reluctantly tagging along—Stu shrugged and noticed she had left her Diet Coke on the pastor's desk. "I imagine it will be pretty hot out there at her prayer meeting."

Everyone suppressed a grin. Toby introduced the pallbearers, most of whom had been at the hospital the night Emma died. Judy and Ashley couldn't help but notice how diverse this group was. Clarence the rapper and Kamisha Whitlock were of African descent. Luis was a plumber from Mexico. Mr. Kim, the grocer, was Korean. The two Caucasians were on opposite ends of the age spectrum. Shauna Cochran, the schoolteacher, was just a year out of college, and Tom McAllister, the retired pilot, was older than Emma.

Toby led the family into the sanctuary and escorted them to their seats on the second row on the left-hand side. Everyone else had already been seated for some time, and the overflow crowd filled the back hallway.

Ashley looked around the room with appreciation. "I like this place," she said, taking in the stained-glass windows and the worn but polished woodwork. She was a girl with an eye for beauty, and to her the old building had a feel of being a holy place yet still accessible to ordinary people.

"Look!" Ashley whispered to her mother, pointing to a set of drums on the stage. "Do they have, like, a band here?"

Her mother just shrugged, clueless about the nuances of church percussion. A thought took hold and began worrying her. What if Marilyn was right? Maybe this church was some kind of cult or something. What if her mother had become mixed up in something bizarre?

A few minutes after ten the funeral director closed the casket, and the service began. A young man with multiple piercings sat down with some African-looking drums next to the trap set, which remained unused during this service. Another guy with a shaved head strapped on a guitar, while two black women took their places at the piano and organ. A slim, pretty Asian woman in her twenties walked up and welcomed the crowd, then invited them to stand and sing. Lyrics appeared on the screen that came down from the ceiling behind her. "These songs are for Emma," she said, "who taught us all how to love."

For almost thirty minutes they sang. A few of the hymns were vaguely familiar to Judy, but most of the music was completely foreign. Stu had an aversion to singing, period, but on the inside, he was feeling the vibe. The tempo went from joyful, even celebrative, to a more personal, intimate tone. Judy glanced over and saw Ashley smiling, doing her best to sing along to songs she'd never heard in her life. A few people raised their hands as they sang; everyone seemed to participate fully. The worship leader closed the time with prayer and invited them to have a seat.

Toby took the stage with no pulpit in front of him. He began his homily in a warm, conversational tone.

"Our friend Emma Estes went home Monday night. She had been with us so long that we kind of forgot that this world was not her home. Emma spent seventy-seven years here—but she will spend an eternity with her Savior!"

At that the congregation broke out in applause. The family sat uneasily, having never experienced anything quite like this.

"The author of Hebrews spoke about people of faith, people like Emma. Hebrews 11:13-16 says, 'All these people were still living by faith when they died. They did not receive the things promised; they only saw them and welcomed them from a distance. And they admitted that they were aliens and strangers on earth. People who say such things show that they are looking for a country of their own. If they had been thinking of the country they had left, they would have had opportunity to return. Instead, they were longing for a better country—a heavenly one. Therefore God is not ashamed to be called their God, for he has prepared a city for them.'"

In spite of her many doubts, Judy's heart swelled with anticipation at the thought of her mother going to a new place. She'd never really thought about her going anywhere. In her mind, *When you're dead, you're dead.* If what Toby was saying was more than just wishful thinking, then maybe, just maybe there would be another opportunity to be with her mother. Another chance to be the daughter she had failed at being in this life.

Stu was also touched by this particular scripture. Surely Marilyn had read it many times, but he had obviously been tuned out. Too bad. This was good stuff. He found a scrap of paper in his pocket and scribbled the biblical reference to look at again later.

Toby continued, "So we gather together this morning to celebrate the homegoing of a mother and a friend, Emma Estes. I think a Christian memorial service is the ultimate act of defiance. The reason we can rejoice in the face of death is that for those of us who, like Emma, have placed our faith in Jesus Christ, death cannot touch us! Satan reaches out for us at the moment of our death, only to find an empty shell in his hands. Our soul—the essence of who we are—is safe in the care of the Savior.

"Death has been defanged and declawed. The grave is no longer a place to be feared since that day almost two thousand years ago when God reached down into a tomb outside Jerusalem and breathed life back into the broken, mutilated body of Jesus Christ. In the resurrection of our Lord, God demonstrated His awesome power—the power to give each one of us an abundant life, a purposeful life, and an eternal life.

"The apostle Paul wrote the Corinthian church saying, 'I declare to you, brothers, that flesh and blood cannot inherit the kingdom of God, nor does the perishable inherit the imperishable. Listen, I tell you a mystery: We will not all sleep, but we will all be changed—in a flash, in the twinkling of an eye, at the last trumpet. For the trumpet will sound, the dead will be raised imperishable, and we will be changed.... "Death has been swallowed up in victory." "Where, O death, is your victory? Where, O death, is your sting?"... But thanks be to God! He gives us the victory through our Lord Jesus Christ.'"

The crowd stayed in sync with the young pastor as he moved to a personal illustration, with several verbalizing their agreement. "Tha's right, Pastor. You go on and tell us now," said the African American lady with the big hat.

"I can remember my mother explaining death to me when my own grandmother died. I must have been around eight years old. A lady at the funeral was expecting a baby. Mom asked me, 'What if that baby could make the choice to stay inside his mother instead of being born? It's all he's ever known. He's safe and warm and never gets hungry. Do you think he would stay where he is?'

"I said, 'No way, Mom! He would want to be born so he could run and play and ride his bike!' My mom then said, 'You're right. And that's the way Christians feel about heaven. We aren't afraid of dying because it's just like being born into another world that's so much better than this one that we can't even begin to describe it.'"

Again the crowd applauded in agreement. Without thinking about it, Stu and Judy joined in.

"But those of us who have yet to join Emma in heaven cannot help but grieve. Not over Emma's gain, but over our loss. Does God's Word offer any help for *us?*"

A chorus of "Yes!" filled the room. Quoting the psalmist, Toby's voice rose with emotion. "The righteous cry out, and the LORD hears them; he delivers them from all their troubles. The LORD is close to the brokenhearted and saves those who are crushed in spirit!"

The lady in the hat stood with her hands toward heaven and gave an impromptu prayer at the top of her lungs. "Thank you, Lawd, that we're not alone in our sufferin'!"

When the room settled down, Toby brought the energy level down just a bit. "Death can be a stark reminder of our own frailty. It was just a few days ago that Emma was with us looking as healthy as ever. It can be fearful to realize how quickly death can come to any one of us.

"If the thought of death brings fear and uncertainty, then Emma would want you to know the same peace and assurance that she had. Jesus said, 'I tell you the truth, whoever hears my word and believes him who sent me has eternal life and will not be condemned; he has crossed over from death to life.'

"Have you crossed over? Have you ever put aside your pride and ambition and said, 'Lord, I give my life to You. Be merciful to me and take away the guilt of my sins. I believe that Jesus died and lived again for my sake. I can't trust myself any longer to run my life, so now I put my trust in You and accept from You the kind of eternal life that Emma Estes knew'?

"A prayer like that will get you started toward living the same abundant, peaceful life that Emma Estes knew. And the same eternal reward will be yours one day as well."

The pastor began his conclusion. "What do you want to be remembered for when you die? The apostle Paul said, 'To me, to live is Christ and to die is gain.' Emma could say that. Can you? Or will we say like so many people these days, 'To me, to live is money...and to die is to leave it all behind. To me, to live is power and influence...and to die is to lose both. To me, to live is fame...and to die is to be quickly forgotten. To me, to live is possessions...and to die is to depart with nothing.' They don't have quite the same ring to them, do they?" A chorus of "No!" rang out.

"You can live for wealth, but you'll always live in fear of losing it. You can live for fame, but you'll always be driven to make yourself look better than you really are. You can live for power and influence, but they will both make you prideful and arrogant. You can live for possessions, but enough is never enough, and greed will be your only reward.

"Why not choose instead a life of serving others and glorifying

God? A life like Emma chose for the last twenty-five years of her life? Everyone who knew Emma knew about her little journal." The crowd laughed and nodded in agreement. Little conversations broke out around the room.

Ashley looked at her mom with anxiety in her eyes. Judy squeezed her hand and whispered, "We'll get it—right after the funeral, honey."

"That little journal helped Emma keep track of what God was doing in her life. She called it her 'Living on Purpose' journal. And we've all been the beneficiaries of her spiritual growth, haven't we?" Again, the crowd smiled as one and voiced their agreement.

"Emma has already triumphed over death because of what Jesus did on her behalf. Wouldn't it be an even greater act of defiance against death if, as a result of Emma's death, someone else began today to change the direction of his life? Wouldn't Emma love that? Wouldn't our Lord love it? His victory can be your victory—in Jesus Christ our Lord."

Toby closed with words of Paul that he said had been Emma's favorite verse: "'The time has come for my departure. I have fought the good fight, I have finished the race, I have kept the faith.'

"Emma challenged me with those words. I'm only thirty-three years old, but almost daily I think about the end of my life and how much I want to be able to speak those words with integrity. Let's follow Emma's example and live life on purpose so that we, too, can die knowing we have fought the good fight, finished the race, and kept the faith. Let's pray."

After the homily, Toby opened the microphone for people to

share stories about how their lives had been influenced by Emma. Stu, Judy, and Ashley alternately cried and laughed as person after person shared a story of how "Miz Emma" had loved and encouraged them. Many reported that they now kept their own journals. Clarence told his story by way of a rap for the crowd. Mr. Kim, who struggled with English, had his daughter, the woman who had led the worship time, interpret for him. The testimonials ran until almost noon, when Pastor Toby wrapped things up with an invitation for people to join them at the cemetery, then meet back at the church for a meal in the fellowship hall.

During his closing prayer, Marilyn slipped back outside from the foyer, where she had entered to escape the heat and eavesdrop on Toby's part of the service.

She had managed to corner most of the people from her own church in the parking lot, but when the sounds of singing continued for longer than most of them had planned on being there, one by one they had made their excuses, given their regrets, and left her alone in the sweltering heat. Including Reverend Lamb. Marilyn was disappointed but not surprised. She'd said nothing, knowing her silence wounded him more than her words.

Marilyn could hardly contain herself on the ride to the graveside service. She had made a big mistake by not sitting in on the service. Now she couldn't criticize it without everyone knowing she'd slipped inside. She tried to fish for something to disparage but got nowhere. The consensus from Judy, Ashley, and that snake Stuart was that the service was quite meaningful, encouraging, personal, and just exactly what their mother had asked for. Even

Marilyn's chilly heart felt a flicker of warmth when she heard Ashley ask her mom if they could come back on Sunday.

After the graveside service, the funeral home's limousine took the family back to the church, where a feast was waiting, prepared by the members of the church. Ham, scalloped potatoes, home-baked rolls, fresh garden produce, and dozens of salads awaited them. Another table nearly buckled under the weight of pies and cakes of every description. Every one of the family—even Marilyn—was surprised to find that they indeed had an appetite, and all enjoyed the food immensely while listening to more first-hand stories of Emma's influence in the lives of the people of this neighborhood.

Chapter Six

I was over at Skeeter's house with the girls after our weekly Bunko game, and we were talking about books we'd read. Everyone else was talking about the trashy romance novels they read. I got to telling about Pilgrim's Progress, how I'd finally read it for myself after all these years of hearing about it. And I just rattled and rattled about how in the book Christian's journey is really every Christian's journey. Everyone was nice, like they were paying attention, but it dawned on me that I was monopolizing the conversation. Worse, I was being a Pharisee. Lord, forgive me for talking too much. Help me become a person whose reputation is that of a listener, not a talker.

Relational goal: Talk less. Listen more. For the next three months, I will not offer my opinion, suggest a solution, or talk just to be talking. Instead I will listen. When the conversation lags, instead of jumping in, I'll say something like, "Tell me more." Maybe if I take into account that the Lord gave me two ears and only one mouth, I'll do more listening and only half as much yakking.

—FROM EMMA'S JOURNAL, NOVEMBER 19, 1982

A s soon as they could get away, Judy and Ashley drove to Emma's house to retrieve the journal. On the way both shared their observations and feelings about the service. While neither could articulate what they had been expecting, both admitted they were pleasantly surprised and feeling better about things than they had in a long time.

Their sense of encouragement vanished when they turned up Longfellow Street and saw the For Sale sign in the front yard.

Ashley jumped out before the car quit rolling. They could tell the draperies had been removed. When she looked in the window, she screamed, "No! No! Where did everything go?"

Judy was right behind her, wishing for the first time in her life that she owned a gun. She grabbed her daughter, and the two of them began to cry in outrage.

"What happened, Mom?"

"I don't know, but I'm sure that Marilyn will know."

Ben went home at noon on Friday because of the pain from his fall the day before. He found the bottle of ibuprofen and picked up his keys to go get a case of cold ones to wash it down. Sunshine was on an overnight retreat with the chorus she sang in at school. As he picked up his keys from the little ledge by the door, he noticed the journal he'd taken from the old woman's estate. *I should take that back,* he thought, embarrassed by his larceny. *Someone will want it to remember her by.* He opened it to that first paragraph he had read yesterday just after he had lost the load of boxes and fallen.

Unwilling to live my life in the future the way I've lived it in the past, I resolve that—submitted to God and with His help—I will become each day more like the person He created me to be.

Something in that sentence felt like a cool breeze on his parched spirit. The promise, the hope contained in just forty words. He flipped through the first page or two, finding what he believed to be quotations from the Bible.

A small dream of possibility came over Ben; he set his keys down, walked over to his chair, and began to read. Some time later he slid from his chair and ended up on his knees in tears, crying out to God.

When he did leave the house several hours later, he came back, not with beer, but with a red spiral notebook. On the cover he wrote "Living on Purpose Journal," and after writing the date, he copied Emma's first paragraph word for word.

Ben had not grown up in church and had only the vaguest understanding of spiritual things. But his helpless spirit made up for his lack of knowledge as he wrote out a prayer to God.

God, whoever and whatever You are. I am at Your mercy. I am powerless to control my life. I've tried, and I keep messing up. I can't stop drinking. I can't get over losing Linda. I can't do anything. Will You help me? I don't deserve Your help. You of all people know how many bad things I've done. But I've heard somewhere that You are merciful and forgiving. If that's true, then here's Your chance, because I am desperate for forgiveness and mercy. Please take control of what's left of my life and fix it. If there's anything left that You can fix, it's Yours. I'll live the rest of my life for You.

He went on to fill a page with some aspirations that just a day earlier would have been impossible. The words didn't even seem his own. Now he felt as though he could not fail. Ben fell on his knees again, not from intoxication, but from the joy of a spirit set free. He didn't have a word for it, but if Emma or Skeeter had been there, they'd have said, "Honey, you just got saved."

Judy didn't trust herself enough to talk with Marilyn face to face, so she called as soon as she got home. Marilyn was at a meeting at her church, and Stu acted as surprised as she and Ashley had been.

"Are you sure? I can't believe Marilyn would do something like this without at least mentioning it to me."

"Trust me. That house doesn't even have a dust bunny left in it. Someone hauled away everything."

"Sis, I don't know what to say. Mom did sign the house over to Marilyn a few years ago, but she should have at least let you—"

"She did what? Why in the world would Mom give her house to Marilyn and not you? Did Mom have a will?"

"You'll have to ask Marilyn. I never thought much about it, to tell the truth. I remember when they did the paperwork. Marilyn said that Mom needed someone to look after her affairs, so she had Mom deed everything over to her, and then Marilyn paid the bills and stuff. Mom gave her power of attorney in case something happened. Marilyn didn't think I could do it. The bills, I mean. And you were kind of out of the picture, you know."

"I know. But this is just too much, even for Marilyn. Listen, I didn't want a thing of Mom's. Today was enough for me to remember her by. But Ashley wanted her journal. She found it when we went over to pick up Mom's dress. It was the only thing of her grandmother's she wanted."

"I'll ask her, but I don't see anything around here. She must have given everything away."

"Well, whatever she did with Mom's things, I want to know immediately when she gets home. She can have any money, all the rest of Mom's things. But I want Ashley to have that journal, and if I have to snatch her baldheaded to get it, I will."

Back on Longfellow Street, the neighbors were as upset as Judy and Ashley had been about the For Sale sign, which had popped up while they were all at the funeral. When the sun began to set, an impromptu block meeting convened on Skeeter Wilson's front porch.

"Feels funny being over on this side of the street after all the years we used to sit and visit across the way. But here's the deal. We gotta do something to help Emma's family, y'all," Skeeter began, her accent flaring up from time to time, even after all these years away from Alabama.

A man on the steps said, "I don't know about that big lady with the skinny husband, but I know that Judy and Ashley are hurtin' for certain and have no one to turn to."

One of Emma's Bunko buddies volunteered to line up people to cook meals and deliver them to the mother and daughter. Ernie, the retired police officer, said if they had a yard, he'd mow it for them—no charge—for the rest of the summer. Rogelio spoke through his wife, Lupe, whose English was better, and volunteered to take care of Judy's car if anything broke down. Luis offered free plumbing services.

Clarence chimed in. "Did y'all hear about that bossy lady having a fit in the pastor's office over the pallbearers Emma picked? She said she wasn't goin' to stay in no church like ours, so she was going to wait outside in the heat."

"She was standin' in the back during the preacher's talk," reported Danny, Skeeter's younger brother. "I seen her." Several raised an eyebrow at this news.

"I sat next to the family at the meal," offered Shauna Cochran. "I could tell they felt out of place, like we knew Emma better than they did."

"I was across the table from Ashley," said Mona, the young worship leader. "She told me that right after the service they were coming over to the house to pick up Emma's journal. She had found it when she was here the other day but didn't get home with it."

"When they came by right after the funeral, they were obviously surprised to see the house empty," said Kamisha Whitlock, who had had to leave the funeral early because of a sick child. "I've got a feeling that Ashley never got her grandmother's journal."

"That big lady was here yesterday. I wonder if…"

"Watch who you're calling big," someone called out good-naturedly from the darkening side of the porch.

"You're right," Skeeter acknowledged. "We all need to watch the way we talk about people. Maybe she can't help being big. But she can sure help being so bossy. You should have heard her yelling at the guys from Helping Hands. Anyway, like I was sayin'—"

"Hey, that's it!" said Kamisha. "*She* was the one who put the house on the market. She wouldn't have cared about Emma's journal. I'll bet Helping Hands has it! Those guys who were moving the stuff—they were just throwing anything and everything in boxes. Are they still open?"

Someone grabbed the Yellow Pages and called, only to discover they were closed for the weekend. Skeeter appointed a task force to be there when they opened Monday morning. No one seemed to notice that she had stepped naturally into the role of neighborhood matriarch, the role Emma had held for as long as anyone could remember. Like Emma's, her leadership came as a by-product of the trust she'd earned by being a friend and a confidante to so many people for so many years.

Skeeter asked Shauna Cochran to start contacting people and have them write down their stories of how knowing Emma had changed their lives. "Then, Shauna, you put them all together in one of those pretty scrapbooks you do so well, and we'll give that to the family."

Turning to the crowd, she said, "Why don't all of you get on the phone tomorrow morning and call that Realtor and see what ol' Crabby-Pants—does anyone remember her name? I've got to get a better attitude toward that woman. Anyway, find out what she's asking for Emma's house. Act like an interested buyer, but whatever price they are asking, let them know it's too much for this neighborhood, then hang up. Here's what we're going to do. Emma had a dream for her house when the day came that…when the day came. We're going to make that dream come to pass."

And what a dream it was. If Skeeter had served double-shot espressos to everyone, they could not have been more buzzed when they finally dispersed around nine. Few slept that night. If they could pull off this impossible dream, Emma's personal ministry of touching lives would go on indefinitely.

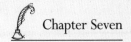
I was so excited to be able to run in that 5K race last week. It's such a big trend these days; "jogging" they call it. Who would have thought that at my age I would be seen jogging in public! But there was a whole crowd of us, young and old, big and small, fast and slow. I was among the slowest, but I did beat that old man with the walker! As thrilling as it was, here's what I discovered: I hate running. So do I have to do it just because everyone else is? Heavens, no.

Physical goal: Walk for thirty minutes, six days a week. Stop and smell flowers, or visit if I feel like it. If the weather's bad, I'll walk at Antioch Mall. I'll see if I can get one of the girls to walk with me for moral support.

—FROM EMMA'S JOURNAL, MAY 6, 1978

When Sunday morning rolled around, Toby was only mildly surprised to see Ashley and Judy in the back row of Graystone Chapel. He spoke easily with them, introducing his wife and their three preschool-age boys. In place of a suit, he was dressed casually in khakis and a short-sleeved polo shirt. Judy was decidedly uncomfortable, fidgeting with her purse and tugging at the hem of her skirt. Several of the women they'd met at the funeral sat with them, and that calmed her a little. Her greatest fear was that some kind of detector would go off with blinking lights and a siren blaring, "Intruder! Intruder!" She was angry with herself for not saying no to Ashley's insistence on coming. But in spite of her nervousness, she felt a building sense of anticipation. Skeeter Wilson stopped by and hugged them both. "I'm working in our preschool ministry this morning, so I won't see you till later, but I want you to come home with me for Sunday dinner."

Judy started to protest. "Oh no, we couldn't—"

"I won't take no for an answer. I want to tell you my story and how Emma changed my life. Besides"—she grinned—"we're having ribs that my brother Danny smoked on the grill and fresh sweet corn from the garden. Who knows? We might even crank up a batch of homemade ice cream." With that, she hurried off to her duty post.

The church was filled to capacity and beyond when, with no warning, the musicians began playing. Everyone stood as if on cue, and four singers with microphones began to lead them in singing. Unlike the funeral, which had a more acoustic feel, this service rocked. Ashley kept grinning at her mother. "Can you believe this?" she mouthed, her voice unheard over the music.

What Judy found more amazing was the participation. One of the lead singers sounded like Aretha Franklin, and the organist had a decidedly Motown groove going on. Though the music was quite appealing to her—she'd grown up on rock-'n'-roll, after all—she was amazed at the number of older adults who were into the music. Afraid to participate, she watched others clap, sway, raise their hands, and close their eyes with intimate looks on their faces. *It's like they are singing a love song to God,* she thought. *Like they know Him personally.*

As the music softened and became quieter, more reflective, Judy tried to picture her mother singing to God the way these people around her were. All at once she remembered several invitations her mother had given to attend Graystone Chapel with her. Never pushy. Never played the guilt card. Therefore Judy never went. As the tears streamed down her face, people nearby hugged her and supplied her with tissues. The tenderness and concern of these strangers pushed her to another round of sobs.

Finally they quit singing and sat down. Before they passed the offering plate, Toby caught her off guard by saying that the offering was for regular attenders and that guests were not expected to participate. *So much for the old "churches always ask for money" excuse,* she thought.

One young woman played a violin solo while a teenage artist sketched pictures of caterpillars and butterflies, winter branches and flowering buds on a huge canvas. When they had both finished, Ashley leaned over and whispered, "What is it?"

"I don't know," Judy whispered back. "But it's beautiful."

"I bet it's about starting over or something."

When Toby stood for the sermon, he said his talk that morning was going to be about "the God of second chances." Judy smiled at Ashley. Toby thanked the artists by name, then explained their unusual duet.

He named the song Alyssa, the violinist, had played. "It's a song written to reflect on the hope of spring after a long winter." He talked about it a little, asking if they caught the subtleties of the tune.

"Umberto's picture shows us that before the butterfly, there is always a caterpillar. Before the crab apple and Bradford pear trees bloom, there are the long days of empty branches, of what looks like death. But when spring comes..."

He announced the Bible passage he'd be speaking from, and Ashley proudly found it in her grandmother's Bible that she had brought along. But when Toby began to read, Ashley was troubled. "This is different," she whispered.

The lady on her other side sensed her confusion. "He's reading from a different translation than your Bible, honey. Yours says the same thing in a little different way. I'll explain later." She smiled as she sat back and patted Ashley's arm.

When the service ended, Judy was shocked to discover that almost two hours had passed. Prior to that day, the thought of a two-hour church service would have ranked right up there with an anesthetic-free root canal.

As they moved toward the door, they were greeted repeatedly with warm smiles and even hugs. "We're praying for you" was as common a phrase from these people as "Have a nice day" was from the clerk at the grocery store.

Skeeter intercepted them before they could leave. In spite of Judy's discomfort at going home with a virtual stranger, she found herself agreeing to follow the old lady's land-yacht sedan from the church to her home.

Chapter Eight

Shauna Cochran told me today that her stepfather, Barney, is dying. Cancer. How I hate that word. But it seems to be a word we hear a lot about these days. Doctors say he could live another six weeks, another six months. But sooner than later, it's going to get him. When Frank's time came, it was so sudden—boom. He was gone. We had no time to prepare. He left nothing. I didn't even know how to write a check. I've wondered if it would be better to know you were going to die or just die. Unfortunately, we don't get to choose. I'm feeling as fit as I've felt in years, but I'm getting old. Time to start preparing for the inevitable. Seems that so many people put off planning for their "homecoming" because they think if they plan it, they might die. I hate to be the one to break it to them, but we're going to die either way.

Relational goal: To get my will up to date and prepare my funeral service and make sure my family does not have to deal with a lot of difficult decisions at my death.

—FROM EMMA'S JOURNAL, MARCH 6, 2001

Since Skeeter's house was right across the street from Emma's, Ashley had tears in her eyes and Judy had a knot in her stomach when the car rolled to a stop. Skeeter hurried to the door to wait for them and passed out another round of hugs as they crossed her threshold. Her brother Danny was much more shy and retreated into the house to start making preparations for lunch. They all followed him into the kitchen. When Ashley looked into the backyard, a beautiful golden retriever looked back at her and started wagging its tail. "Can I go see your dog?" Ashley asked, looking to Skeeter for permission.

"Well, that's Danny's dog, and I don't—"

"That's my dog," Danny declared proudly as he stepped out of the kitchen. "Her name is Lady, and she loves me. But you can go talk to her if you want to." Ashley looked to her mother, who nodded, and she walked outside with Danny talking as if he'd known her all his life.

"Danny's a little slow," Skeeter said, "but he's got a gentle heart. He's usually kinda protective about Lady, but he's sure warmed up to Ashley. Sit down here in this chair, Judy, and visit with me while I get everything ready. It won't take us a minute, and we'll be ready to eat."

Sitting where she could keep an eye on Ashley in the backyard, Judy took a deep breath and blurted out what was on her mind. "Skeeter, why was everyone at church so nice to us today?"

Skeeter laughed and started to make a joke out of it until she realized Judy was serious. Her mouth opened, but her mind had not yet found an answer. "Why, dear, what other way would we be?"

"Judgmental, standoffish, I don't know. I had it in my mind that all churchgoers were like my sister-in-law, but your church seems so...so different."

"Well..." Skeeter paused to think while she slid the ribs Danny had smoked the day before in the oven to heat up. "I guess you are right that some so-called Christians are pretty self-righteous. I hate to say it, but if you'd been at our church even ten years ago, it might not have been the same place. It was your mother who made the difference."

"How so? I mean, the last few days have been a mystery to me. I hear everyone talk as though Emma Estes was Mother Teresa or something, and I hate to admit this, but…I just didn't know that side of her."

"Who did you know?"

"I don't know. Someone else. The mother I grew up with wasn't a religious person. She was an overweight, slightly depressed, shy woman who kept to herself. I know that she got religion some time after Daddy died, and she lost a bunch of weight. But I could never bring myself to find out what happened to her."

"My goodness, child, why not?"

"Well, I was always such a disappointment to her. I divorced… I was…" Sensing in this woman a safe recipient for her shameful secrets, Judy opened the floodgates and told her about Chuck, her divorce, and her life that followed, while the older woman fussed around the kitchen, pausing at times to nod warmly and wipe away tears with the kitchen towel over her shoulder.

By the time Danny and Ashley came inside, lunch was ready, and Judy felt as though the weight of twenty-five years had been lifted from her shoulders. She had even considered discussing her father and the abuse he had brought upon his family, but enough was enough.

"Mrs. Wilson," Ashley said as she wiped her mouth, "that was the best meal I ever ate."

"Call me Skeeter, like everyone else does, honey. My daddy gave me that name. He said I was always buzzing around wanting something. Anyways, you can thank Danny for the ribs. He really knows how to slow smoke them."

"Thanks, Danny," she said, smiling at him across the table. Danny's shyness may have kept him from acknowledging the compliment, but it was evident her words pleased him. Judy added her thanks as well. Danny got up from the table and disappeared to go check on the ice-cream freezer.

"Skeeter, has your church always been so cool?"

"Well, I guess it depends on what you mean by 'cool.' It has definitely changed, and for a long while, I'll tell you, it was a sore spot for a lot of us."

"What do you mean?"

"Honey, you've got to understand that I grew up in Alabama. Alabama Baptist. We sang hymns on Sunday morning and a little Southern gospel on Sunday nights. But we sure never had no rock-'n'-roll. That was the devil's music.

"In a world where everything changed, the church was the one place that never changed. For as long as anyone could remember, the service was exactly the same."

"So why *did* you change?" Judy finally asked.

"Your mama mostly. I don't know how many times she

brought neighbors to church, then they'd never come back. None of the rest of us thought too much of it, but it really bothered Emma.

"Finally when old Pastor Collins retired—he must have been almost eighty—we had to find a new pastor. Your mama stood up at the meeting and said, 'Take a good look around.' We did, not noticing anything unusual. Then she started in. 'We are a dying church,' she told us. 'A bunch of self-centered old people.' That got our attention, I'll tell you what! She said, 'Our children have grown and left us. Why is that? Why are there no young families in our church? They are in our neighborhoods. I see their children playing in the street. They come to my house and visit. But they won't come to our church more than once because they take one look around and know they don't fit in. They don't understand our old-fashioned music. They don't understand our preacher and his theological vocabulary. They know we look at them funny because of the color of their skin.'

"I'm telling you, Emma let us have it that night. Told us we were never going to reach the neighborhood as long as we kept the church out of their reach. What we needed, she said, was a young pastor who could help us change, who could help us reach the young people."

"That's when Toby came?" asked Judy.

"Yep. And boy, did he have his hands full. A few of the old-timers left mad, some died mad, some are *still* mad, but Toby was determined to reach the young folks. And he did. He did it because your mama was always challenging us old folks to put aside our

personal preferences so our church could live for another genera-
tion. Somewhere along the line, we realized that she was right.
Most of us anyways. There are still some who gripe. I tell 'em like
Emma told 'em, 'Just turn off your hearing aid if you don't like it
loud.'"

Danny returned to the room with a little book clutched to his
chest. He sat down at his place and began looking at it. Ashley and
Judy wondered what it was. Skeeter said, "Danny, do you want to
tell these girls about your journal?"

"This is my journal," he said. "I write down stuff to make me
be nicer. Like don't be mean to people who look at my dog. Stuff
like that."

"My grandma had a journal," said Ashley. "I found it and was
going to keep it to remember her by, but someone came and took
everything in the house, including the journal."

"Honey, we're going to do everything we can think of to help
you find that journal. I'm guessing it's at Helping Hands. Their
truck was by here the other day and loaded up everything. First
thing tomorrow morning we'll go down and look for it."

"This is my journal," Danny repeated, not wanting to be left
out of the conversation.

"Did you know my grandma?" Ashley asked.

Danny nodded vigorously. "Miz Estes was my friend. She's the
one who told me, 'Danny, you be like Jesus and get a book to write
stuff.'"

Puzzled, mother and daughter turned for explanation to
Skeeter, who was laughing.

"Seems like everyone who knew Emma ended up keeping a journal. She never told you about it? Well, I can't explain it like she did, but it had to do with a verse of Scripture Emma found right after she turned her life over to Jesus. It's at the end of the Christmas story in Luke's gospel. 'And Jesus grew in wisdom and stature, and in favor with God and men.' Luke 2:52, I think it is. That verse sums up Jesus' life from the time he was twelve until he began his public ministry around the age of thirty."

"How does everyone know all this stuff from the Bible?" Judy interrupted. "I've heard more Bible in the past two weeks than in my whole life. Am I the only one around who hasn't read it?"

Skeeter laughed. "Not at all, dear. It's just that we study the Bible because God gave it to us so we could live without regrets."

What would that kind of life be like? thought Judy.

"What about the verse?" Ashley asked as she watched Danny flipping through his little notebook.

"I'm sorry, honey. I get off track so easily. Well, this phrase, 'And Jesus grew in wisdom and stature, and in favor with God and men,' just really struck Emma. She thought it was the secret to life. If people could be intentional about growing in wisdom, they wouldn't keep repeating the same mistakes.

"The part about Jesus growing in stature meant physical fitness to Emma. She thought if she was intentional about growing healthier in her body, she'd have the time and energy to make her life count. Which she proved to be true, I might add. Mercy, that woman had the energy of a fifteen-year-old boy.

"H'm, let's see, what comes next? Oh yes, growing in favor with

God. Emma knew she couldn't make God love her more or less than He already does; that's not what it's about. It meant for her that she could get to know the Lord, close and personal-like. Could she pray? I'll say she could. She could talk with Jesus as if He were sitting right there on the couch, and she could hear Him speak to her. That was why people had to listen to her. When she spoke, we knew it came out of those long times of conversation with the Lord, and who wanted to argue with that?"

"Wait a minute," Judy interrupted again. "I don't want to be cynical here, but are you saying that my mother could hear God speak? That sounds a little far-fetched to me."

"I never heard her say that she heard a voice out loud. But she knew the Bible frontward and backward. I guess that's the main way God spoke to her. But I also think she just knew in her heart what was from God and what was not. When she spoke, you could sense that she knew Him in a real personal way."

"What's the last part mean?" Ashley asked, determined to keep the conversation on track.

"'Jesus grew...in favor with God and men.' That last part was about friends. Emma thought the secret to life was being the kind of friend that everyone wants to have. And she was. There's not a person on this block who doesn't know her by name. Who hasn't a story to tell about how she made a difference during some crisis in their life. And the flip side of that was, everyone wanted to be Emma's friend. Me included."

"I still don't get the part about the journal," Ashley said.

"Oh. Right. Honey, it's hard for old women to answer a simple question. We have to start every story back at the beginning of time, you know. Emma wrote that verse in that little leather journal you found. Then she would set a simple goal in each of those four areas: Intellectual, that's 'wisdom.' Physical, that's 'stature.' Spiritual, that's 'favor with God.' And Relational, that's 'favor with man.'

"She did this for years without telling anyone. But sure as shootin', that quiet little woman who lived across the street from us began to change. Every few months she'd write a goal in each of the four categories. Just a little goal or a little step to take. She said if she couldn't do it, it was too big, and she'd break it down to something simple. When that little step became a habit, she'd take another step.

"She read more books than a college professor. She started walking every day, rain or shine. She read her Bible till the cover fell off. She prayed till she had calluses on her knees. And she began bein' a friend to us all."

Skeeter took Judy's hand. "That's why everyone loved your mama." Judy dabbed at the tears with her dinner napkin. "Are you okay, hon?"

"I'm fine," she lied, pulling herself together. "I just wish I'd known the woman everyone else knew. I can't believe that I'm her only daughter, and everyone else knew her better than I did."

Skeeter continued to hold her hand, searching for the right words. "Well, you can't change the past, girl, but you can change the future."

"What do you mean?"

"That's what Emma's life was all about. Her life really didn't start until after she turned fifty. It was after her husband, your daddy, died that she turned her life over to God. She believed He gave her that Bible verse to live by. She called it 'living on purpose.' That's why everyone who knew her started keeping their own 'Living on Purpose' journal. Like Danny. He can't spell real good, but he gets the gist of the idea. And it's changed him as well.

"Em used to say the biggest mistake most people make is just going through life without paying attention." Skeeter laughed. "I'd have to say that Emma Estes paid attention to how to live life more than anyone I ever knew."

Several other people at that table were beginning to pay attention as well.

Chapter Nine

Ahora he estado tomando las lecciones españolas por seis meses. Esta
noche, estoy teniendo Rogelio y su familia encima para la cena.
Hablaremos en español, nada inglés.

I have been taking Spanish lessons for six months now. Tonight
I am having Rogelio and his family over for dinner. We will talk
in Spanish, no English. I hear people say that people who move
here to America from someplace else should learn English, and I
think that's true. But until that happens, how will they get along?
What if one of their children gets sick and the doctor doesn't speak
their language? What if they need help getting a driver's license or
filling out a job application? I want them to know that at least one
ol' gal cares enough about them to learn their heart language.
Who knows, maybe I can share about Jesus with them in Spanish
as well.

Spiritual goal: Buy a Spanish Bible, and have my devotions in
Spanish for the next three months.

—FROM EMMA'S JOURNAL, CINCO DE MAYO (MAY 5), 1984

O n Monday morning Ben arrived for work fifteen minutes
early. As he drove in, he reflected on his weekend. After his
life-changing encounter with the journal and with God, his daughter had arrived home from her chorus trip late Saturday afternoon.

They had dinner together, then talked until well after midnight. Ben admitted his alcoholism and asked her forgiveness. This was his first relational goal in his "Living on Purpose" journal.

The next morning, Sunday, Sunny had been shocked to be awakened by her father saying, "Get up. We're going to church." His first spiritual goal was to find out more about the God who had picked him up off the floor of the living room after he had read Emma's journal.

Unfortunately, church had been a pretty disappointing experience that morning. With virtually no background at that sort of thing, Ben had picked the congregation they attended because its architecture gratified the artist in him. Inside the beautiful building, a handful of sad people had endured a dirge of organ music and a sermon read by a man who looked to Ben as though he also would have been happier at home that morning.

That afternoon he had continued to shock Sunny by asking her to take a walk with him, his first physical goal. It had lasted all of fifteen minutes, but afterward, as he lay on the couch watching the baseball game, he had felt proud of himself for making the effort. *Every day,* he had told himself. *Just get off your butt for a little while every day.*

As he had watched the game, he had thought of his first intellectual goal, turned off the television, and picked up the book on being a single parent that he'd bought. *I could write a book on how not to be a dad,* he had thought, marveling at how Sunny was turning into a neat kid in spite of his screwups.

As Ben pulled into the parking lot behind Helping Hands, he

wondered for the hundredth time if what had happened to him was going to last. *Please, God,* he prayed as he walked to the loading dock, *help me not to blow it all up today.*

When he walked into the office to get his itinerary for the day, his heart stopped at Rita's first words. "When you loaded up the stuff from that house on Longfellow Street, did you see a little book covered in red leather with handwriting inside?"

Avoiding the answer, Ben commented, "There was a lotta stuff in that old lady's house."

"Well, I had three voice-mail messages waiting for me this morning, and two more people came by looking for that old lady's journal. Seems that none of the rest of the family knew the contents of the house were being donated to us. The lady you met at the house? She was the daughter-in-law. Her husband didn't even know what she was up to. He was one of the ones who called about the journal. The neighbor lady across the street wants it, she says, so she can give it to the daughter. Then the daughter herself called, and she wants it. Everyone wants it. Must have a map for buried treasure in it or something."

Ben thought, *That's not far from the truth,* but kept quiet.

Rita got up from behind the desk and handed Ben a computer printout. "Here's your schedule. Lots of little stops today. I'm going to look through the book section one more time and see if I can find that journal. Have a good day, Ben."

As quick as that, Ben was off the hook—except with his conscience. He got in his truck and headed out, not sure what he was going to do. The thought of giving up the book that had turned his life around frightened him. Having Emma Estes's journal felt like...an insurance policy. If he ever had doubts about whether he could change, all he had to do was read it again. There, in delicate script, was the evidence that someone else had done it.

But if it meant that much to him, what would it mean to the family? *A beer would sure help me think.*

Marilyn closed the door to her office and called Barry Lamb at home. Monday was his day off.

"It's me," she said as he answered. "Can you talk?"

"Yes, but you know I don't like it when people call on my day off."

"I'm not just 'people,' am I? I wanted to tell you how much I enjoyed your message yesterday. Besides, can't a board member call her pastor just to say she needs to hear your voice?"

"You sound uncharacteristically needy this morning, Marilyn."

"I don't know what that's supposed to mean, but I do need you, you know that." She let the flirt linger for a moment, then added, "What would I do without my pastor?"

"You don't need anyone. You have a nice husband, a good life, lots of money. What could you possibly want from me?"

"You are a spiritual man, Pastor. Stuart is not. Besides, he is pulling away from me. I can feel it. You and I communicate on a deeper level. We understand the things of a more spiritual nature."

"All I know is that the more time we spend together, the less spiritual things become. You frighten me."

"And you should be frightened. I'm a strong, passionate woman who gets what she wants."

"Don't talk like that. Please don't do this."

Marilyn glanced at the clock. Time for her manicure. "Good-bye, Benny."

"Barry."

"What?"

"My name is Barry, not Benny."

"Of course. How stupid of me. Good-bye, Bar…Reverend Lamb."

Benny. A name she hadn't spoken aloud in years. Not since her junior year at Baylor University in Texas. Her father, Charles Symmes, had driven to Waco to see her. Marilyn was elated. When she was a child, Charles had always been too busy with his oil deals to give her or his wife or son any of his valuable time. When he did speak, it was only to criticize their weight or their wardrobes.

His secretary had instructed her to meet her father at Porter's Steakhouse. When she arrived, he stood to greet her, giving her a peck on the cheek. Also standing with him was an attractive young man whom he introduced as Benny Kinsey. Benny, her father told her, was also a Baylor student. Benny's father owned the bank that kept Charles afloat with his boom-and-bust-cycle business. Since the fathers were such close friends, Charles had said, it seemed that their children should at least know each other. After all, they were both at Baylor, and... The oil man grinned. "Look at me, always wheelin' and dealin'. Let's order us some steaks and visit for a while."

From that day until just months before graduation, Marilyn and Benny were a couple. Marilyn was attracted to him for a number of reasons. He was tall, handsome, and funny. An outstanding tennis player. And he loved God. That was his distinguishing characteristic.

Not so her own family. Her father was a blasphemous man, her mother interested in her bridge games at the country club and maintaining appearances, even when a bad hunch in the oil patch had sent their financial worth into the red.

Unlike some of the "preacher boys" on campus, Benny, with his winsome personality, kept his zeal from becoming obnoxious. Marilyn wanted two things—to be worthy of Benny's love and to be worthy of God's love as well.

If Marilyn had ever really heard about God's unconditional love, she must have considered herself the exception. So she began in college the patterns and habits of the striver—working to be better, more religious, more worthy. Grace was a fuzzy concept, mercy something for the weak. Marilyn was fiercely determined never to be weak. She would become a spiritual giant if it killed her.

On the inside, something did indeed begin to die the day she began that journey.

On the outside, she quickly adopted the mannerisms and

vocabulary of others at the Baptist Student Union. Benny treated her well and was always kind and gentle. When he never moved toward her in demonstrations of intimacy, she attributed it to his desire for moral purity.

After he proposed in October of their senior year, she was euphoric for months. But the euphoria dissipated in an instant one cold March afternoon just nine weeks prior to their wedding date.

"I can't do this," said Benny.

"Do what, dear? Walk to the library?"

"No… Marilyn, sit down. There's something I've got…I need to tell you. Your dad told me if I would… I can't marry you."

The last clear phrase of his stammer caught her like a fist in the diaphragm, taking with it even the hope of breath. She sat stunned, waiting for the fatal blow.

"I can't live with myself if I don't break this off right now. Marilyn, you are a wonderful girl. But I don't love you. Your father set this up. I thought I could love you eventually, but I can't do this. We're going to start a new church after college, and your father said he'd finance us to get started, and—"

"My father? What are you saying? My father told you to marry me?"

"It's not exactly like that. He just thought you'd make a great pastor's wife and that we'd all be happy, but…"

Marilyn pulled the beautiful marquise diamond off her finger, flung it at Benny's face, and never spoke to him again. That had been well over twenty-five years ago.

A knock on her office door jarred Marilyn from her trip back to a painful memory, but its effect lingered on her mood all day long.

At Highland Hills Middle School, two seventh-grade girls bumped into each other in the hall. "Sorry," they said simultaneously.

"Aren't you, like, in Ms. Lieberman's honors algebra?" asked the first.

"Well, yeah," said the other. "Your name is Sunshine, right?"

"Yeah. It's weird, I know. My parents were, like, hippies or something. What's your name?"

"Ashley. Did you understand what Ms. Lieberman was talking about today?"

"About slope? Sort of."

"If you have the coordinates negative three over four, when you're plotting it, do you go down three and to the left four, or down three and to the right four?"

"Down three and to the right four, or up three and to the left four," said Sunny. "I know, it's weird."

"Are you going to lunch now? Do you think I could ask some more questions? I've been zoned out lately." She smiled apologetically. "My grandma died."

"Oh, I'm sorry. Sure I can help you. Not that I know what's going on all the time. Maybe we can figure it out together." The two girls headed off toward the cafeteria, not knowing how intertwined their lives were about to become.

The phone rang yet again at Hearth and Home Realty. For the seventh or eighth time in the last hour, Jerry Sullivan heard his secretary, Alvena, describe the old house they had just listed at 411 Longfellow Street. He got up from his desk and walked to hers and listened in.

"Yes, that home is a three-bedroom, Craftsman-style home built in the 1930s. Large lot, fenced backyard, one-car detached garage. It has been immaculately kept and is listed for seventy-four thousand dollars."

There was a pause as the other person spoke. "Yes ma'am. I do understand. But Mr. Sullivan listed the home at that price based on what similar homes in the neighborhood are going for.

"No ma'am. The house has been on the market less than a week. Yes ma'am. If you'd like to look at the house, you can always make a counteroffer. Would you like to set up a time to… Hello? Hello?

"She hung up," Alvena said to her boss. "Sure are a lot of people calling about that place. Everyone says it's too much money. No one wants to take a tour."

"Neighbors calling, I'd guess," said Jerry. "Though why they think it's too much, I don't understand. Most people want to know the houses around them are selling high. Makes their own property values better. Ten years ago that house wouldn't have been worth half what it's listed for. But that area is really turning around.

"A friend of mine on the police force told me crime in that

neighborhood is as low as in some of the more affluent suburbs. No one knows why. Those houses are old but well made. Lots of younger people are moving in and renovating them. All kinds of ethnic backgrounds, which is something you usually don't see. This house is worth every penny of seventy-four thousand. In fact, I'd have probably listed it higher, but the lady who is selling wanted it to move quickly."

Rita dialed the first number on the pink slip of paper and waited for the answer.

"Hello?" answered Skeeter.

"Mrs. Wilson, this is Rita Vallejos at Helping Hands Ministries. I wanted to let you know that we've looked through all the things donated from Mrs. Estes's home, and we have not seen the book you were looking for. I'm so sorry."

"Well, thanks for looking. That book has a lot of sentimental value to some folks, and we were sure hoping it would turn up. Thanks for your time. Good-bye now."

Rita looked at the next name and number of people who had called about the journal and began dialing again.

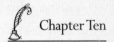

Chapter Ten

Dr. Foster just asked me flat-out at my annual physical, "What is it you like about being overweight?" I looked at him like he was nuts. "Nothing," I said. "Then why don't you do something about it?" he said. I had no answer for him.

Frank's death more than a year ago continues to hurt, but I have more good days than bad days now. When I think of him, the emotion I feel most often is fear. Not fear of him, although I had plenty of that. No, what I feel is the fear that I will die without having really lived. He was a good man in many ways. If only he'd had someone to teach him how to drain off all the anger he carried around...

Anyway, this last year has been a year of growth in many ways. Keeping this journal is really making me think about the choices I have to change my life. But the weight, the weight is the big one, no pun intended.

Physical goal: I will start attending the weight management class that the hospital offers for seniors. I will lose at least thirty-five pounds this year and <u>keep it off for the rest of my life.</u>

—FROM EMMA'S JOURNAL, AUGUST 25, 1977

As the weeks went by, everyone eventually gave up hope of ever finding the journal. Emma's memory remained dear to those who knew her well and elusive to those who didn't.

The neighbors continued their little scheme to delay the sale of Emma's house. Whenever the Realtor's green Lexus SUV pulled into the drive, anxieties went up. Clarence, the would-be rapper, was on call to walk by the house looking like a troublemaker whenever someone came to view the property. The Mexican family next door would turn their stereo as loud as it would go, the accordion sounds of ranchero music reaching out to potential buyers. Once, as a middle-aged couple came out to inspect the back porch after seeing the inside, a couple of teenagers from Graystone Chapel youth group even pretended to sell drugs to one another in the alley. Instead of drugs, they passed along a sandwich bag containing baking soda that Jorge's mother needed to finish making *bizcochitos*.

The scheme seemed to be working. Fewer and fewer people came to see Emma's old home.

While they stalled, waiting for the price to come down, Skeeter had placed Shauna Cochran, the schoolteacher, in charge of phase two, collecting money from all those who had loved Emma. If this coalition of friends and neighbors could raise enough to purchase the home, they would then be able to fulfill one of Emma's last dreams.

It was another Monday morning, and Stu sat praying the whole time that Marilyn read aloud her daily dose of Scripture. *God, don't let me be a coward.* He looked around the richly furnished formal living room. These devotionals were the only time he came into this room. He was afraid to sit on the furniture. He dared not bring a cup of coffee in here, although Marilyn had her ever-present soft drink at hand. He was even afraid to walk through for fear of breaking something. He eyed a porcelain vase on a pedestal in the corner and wondered if he had ever seen it before. Marilyn handled all their finances. He wasn't sure how much their mortgage was or how much they had in savings. He had a lot to learn quickly.

When Marilyn finished reading and told him to pray, Stu bowed his head, but the rote prayer evaporated. He sat in silence, his head bowed, feeling her eyes boring a hole in the top of his skull. He looked up and met her eyes.

"Marilyn, it wasn't right for you to give all Mom's stuff away without letting Judy have a chance to get what she wanted." The sound of his voice was deeper and stronger than he expected. So far so good.

Still unaccustomed to Stu's growing ability to confront her, Marilyn was speechless for a few seconds. Stu unfortunately took this as a hopeful sign. The bonfire of her rage had been started back in college by her fiancé, Benny, and her father. That rage had grown over the years, fueled by every petty grievance, every lack of compliance, every disappointment.

On this day, the firestorm was about to erupt. The hot words started somewhere in her spleen, building like a fireball until they burst forth from her lips.

"How dare you criticize me! You little worm! For the last twenty-five years I've taken care of first you, then your sons, and now your mother—all by myself." She paused, her lip trembling as rage became intertwined with self-pity. "And with not a word of thanks! You are so ungrateful!

"I'm the one who's been there for her. I'm the one she confided in. I'm the one who gave her the idea to give away her old junk so none of us would be bothered by it. I'm the one she trusted enough to take care of her estate. Not you. And certainly not that slut Judy. Don't you dare sit there and tell me what's right or wrong!"

As she paused to catch her breath, Stu looked as if he might respond. Marilyn began the second assault before he could.

"I don't know what's gotten into you lately, *Stuart,* but I won't have it. You embarrassed me at the funeral home, then again at the pastor's office the day of the funeral. I can't believe I'm the one who had to stand up for what was right that day. Where was *your* sense of principle? Why didn't you speak out against those…those *people* your mother wanted for pallbearers? Good heavens, if you had any sense at all of what is *proper,* you'd have been the one to take a stand, and I wouldn't have had to. But no, you always sit back and expect me to take the lead. I have to be the one to hold the standard." Once again self-pity infused her tone. "I get so tired of being the spiritual head of this family when that is supposed to be your job. I would hate to be in your shoes on Judgment Day! You'll have some answering to do!"

"Marilyn—"

"I'm not finished yet. I'm tired of your timidity. I'm tired of your silence. I'm sick of your stupid ham radio and your stupid history books stacked up everyplace. Why can't you be a man for a change?"

Stu decided the only strategy left to hold back the wildfire of her anger was to start a fire of his own.

"Shut up! Just shut up! I've had it with your mouth! I've had it with your self-righteousness! I've had it with your bossy attitude, and I've had it with all this…this bull about how you've been taking care of my mother!"

On Marilyn's forehead a vein bulged.

"My mom took care of herself, okay? For years you've told people you were taking care of her so that everyone at church would think you're a saint. Well guess what, Marilyn. It didn't work. Everyone knows you're a hypocrite. Everyone knows you're a phony. There are some who are scared of you because you're a bully, but everyone knows that there's nothing spiritual about you. You use the God-talk as part of your act.

"We've sat here every morning for almost, what, twenty-five years? Twenty-five years of Bible reading, and you are still mean as the devil. You gossip. You criticize anybody and everybody. You hold grudges forever. You've never forgiven anybody in your life. You're so full of bitterness and hatred that your very soul is full of poison. And worst of all, you stole my mother's home and things!"

"Why, you—"

"Shut up. I'm not through. Because of you, our boys won't have anything to do with the church. Because of you, they picked colleges as far from home as possible. Because of you, they will never come back here to live. Because of you, I haven't been able to have a decent relationship with my one and only sister. And by the way, Judy is no slut. She's a broken person who has known little love or joy in her life. And I intend to do everything I can from this day forward to help her find it."

"Well, haven't you suddenly become the brave little fellow? Standing up to me. Standing up for little sister. I suppose you think that makes you a man."

Stu could not sustain the emotional pitch of his tirade any longer, but he returned to his calm, rational self with a new determination.

"Marilyn, your insults have no effect on me anymore. I'm through with you. I moved most of my things out yesterday afternoon while you were at yet another meeting at church. I'm leaving. For good. I hope you enjoy the rest of your vicious life alone."

Stu got up from his chair and headed for the garage while Marilyn sat there red faced, mouth hanging open, completely incapable of a comeback. He shut the door behind him, and only then did he pump his fist as though he'd just won the Masters and whisper, "Yes!"

Toby Barnes had a full afternoon scheduled at his little office at Graystone Chapel. At three o'clock he greeted Skeeter Wilson.

"Pastor, when Emma met with you to discuss her funeral, did she say anything about her house? We were all shocked when that daughter-in-law gave away all her things and put it on the market so fast."

"I've racked my brain trying to remember, Skeeter. That letter of instruction about her funeral was typical; you know how she was. Emma lived each day as though it was the last day and made plans as though she were going to be around another fifty years.

"I've wondered if she had some sort of premonition about dying, if that's what prompted the letter. But then I think, if that was the case, why didn't she have a will? Why didn't she leave better instructions about the disposal of her things? And why did she deed the house over to her daughter-in-law of all people? You know what she wanted to do with that house," said Skeeter.

"Oh, I know. She talked about it all the time. My guess is that she simply deeded her property over to her daughter-in-law out of convenience so she had more time to devote to her causes. Maybe Emma's plans for the house came after that. I don't know. I won't speculate about the daughter-in-law. I don't even know her. I guess I could talk to her though and find out, but it feels really awkward. I mean, this is the family's business now."

Skeeter fumed. "And it may be that Emma told the daughter-in-law about her plans, and she just ignored them. She's mean, that one. Several people who were late for the funeral said she was outside in the heat, praying real loud, like some kind of Old Testament prophet, that God would bring wrath on this church. You watch out for her, Pastor. She'll bite you, she will."

Toby laughed. "Thanks for your concern. If I run into her, I'll be careful."

"Well, if we have anything to do with it, we'll buy it back from that woman and make Emma's wish come true."

"How much do you have so far?"

"Around seven thousand. It's a poor neighborhood—a lot of people on fixed incomes. I don't know if we can do it or not, but we're going to give it a shot."

"Let me talk to the missions committee and recommend that the church get involved. We don't have much money to put into the house, but if we brought it under the umbrella of our ministry, you wouldn't have to fool with incorporating as a nonprofit. In the meantime…" Toby pulled out his wallet and from behind the photos of his children retrieved a fifty-dollar bill, which he handed to Skeeter.

"My mom gave me this for my birthday. I was saving it for a fishing trip, but I'd much rather be a part of what you are doing. Skeeter, you are following in Emma's footsteps, you know that? God will use you greatly if you let Him."

Skeeter blushed. "Thanks, Pastor. The Lord knows I can't fill Emma's shoes, but someone had to pick up the slack she left. I don't think anybody realized just how involved she was in so many different things. By the way, have you seen Judy and Ashley lately? We had them over for dinner after church that Sunday they were here but haven't seen them since. I've left messages at her house, but she doesn't return my calls."

"As a matter of fact, I'm meeting with Judy in about thirty minutes," said Toby.

"Here at the church? Oh my. That's great, I think. Is everything all right?"

"As far as I know. Just pray for her. I really think God is about to touch her in a special way."

A half-hour later Toby looked up from the sermon in progress on his desk. "Hi, Judy. It's great to see you again. How's Ashley doing?"

Judy avoided eye contact with Pastor Toby, afraid his gentle face might trigger her tears. "Oh, she's fine. Doing really well in school. She's smart, not a dummy like I was." She looked around the office, amazed by all the books. "Have you read all these books?"

"Well, most of them. Some of them are for sermon research— Bible commentaries and such—so I can't say I've read those cover to cover. But I do like books. Do you like to read?"

"Some. Romance novels and stuff." Feeling uncomfortable, she clarified, "Not the real trashy ones. It's just a diversion, something to keep me occupied. Better than television, I guess."

"I agree with you there. Say, before we get to whatever it is you want to talk about, I'd be interested in hearing your first impressions from when you attended our church a few weeks ago."

"Well, that's sort of what I wanted to talk about. I…I really liked the service. It was different from what I expected…"

"What were you expecting?"

"I'm not sure. Traditions, I guess. Bowing and kneeling and stuff. I don't know. But I wasn't expecting to be…" Her eyes misted. Toby pushed a box of tissues toward her and waited for her to continue.

Dabbing and sniffling, finally blowing and wiping, Judy regained her voice. "It's just that all my life I've felt like an outsider. In high school I was never part of the popular crowd. I hung out with what the other kids called 'the freaks.' That was in the late sixties, early seventies. I got into some stuff that caused a lot of hurt and anxiety with my parents." Judy went on to tell Toby an abridged version of her past.

"What's funny is that for years I haven't talked to anyone about this stuff. In the past few weeks, I've found myself telling anyone who will listen. I even told Ashley, at least most of it. She'd never known about her dad. I had always just avoided her questions. I told Skeeter Wilson, who I don't even know that well. I don't know why I'm able to talk about it all of a sudden. But it's not as bad as I thought it would be.

"But this church made me feel, I don't know, like I was accepted. And I've never felt that before. Even at work. I've been at the post office for almost thirty years now, and I don't have any real friends there. I can't seem to get into whatever inner circle it takes to get promoted. My neighbors don't know me. My family...well, you've seen how close we are."

The tears began dribbling down her cheeks again. "But this church, it feels like you love me. But you don't know me, and if you did..." Her tears turned into sobs. Judy's shoulders heaved with the rejection of the years, the sorrows of a lifetime. Toby just let her cry, reaching over occasionally to pat her shoulder. After almost ten minutes, she began to feel relief. "I'm sorry. I usually don't fall apart like that."

"No need to apologize. This is a safe place to cry. Are you ready to talk? If you are, I'd like to respond to a couple of things you said."

She nodded her head.

"First, I can't tell you how glad I am to hear you say you feel accepted here. That's the exact atmosphere I believe a church ought to have. There's an old cliché that says, 'The church is a hospital for sinners, not a Hall of Fame for saints.'"

Judy smiled. "I like that."

"Most of the people who now attend our church did not grow up in church, or if they did, they were hurt as a result. So when you say, 'If we only knew about your past,' you're wrong. All the people here have a past they'd rather forget. Everyone here has baggage. Everyone here has received hurt and given hurt, including me. We're all broken, all needy. And we haven't forgotten that.

"Very few people here would be surprised or shocked by your story. What you'd find instead would be more of what you've already found—acceptance. This is a safe place, Judy. A place to be who you are and be loved as a result."

"I love the idea of that. But how can that be true?"

Toby began to get excited. "See, that's at the heart of the gospel of Jesus. 'All have sinned' is one verse, but it goes along with 'God so loved the world that he gave his one and only Son.' This whole thing is about God's unconditional love—in spite of our short-comings, in spite of our rebellion, in spite of our self-focus. And Jesus said over and over again, 'As I have loved you, so you must love one another.' So that means there is no place in the church for self-righteousness, smugness, or—"

"You mean like my sister-in-law, Marilyn."

"I don't know Marilyn, but if that's the way she is, she's been deceived. You can't win God's favor by being better than anyone else. 'Cause even if you succeeded, you'll still fall short of being as good as God. If she ever got it clear in her own mind that God loves the most disgusting criminal just as much as he loves her, she couldn't stay the way she is any longer. But let's forget about Marilyn for now and talk about you."

Judy sighed. "There's not much to talk about. I'm a lonely, depressed, divorced woman who uses food like she used to use drugs. When I quit smoking marijuana after Ashley was born, I took up ice cream and Sara Lee pound cake with chocolate syrup.

"I really liked this church, but I'm not a religious person, so I felt like a phony when I was here that Sunday."

"Judy, what I'm trying to tell you is, *forget about religion.* Religion is about trying to earn God's love by doing good deeds. This is about *relationship.* See, God loves you unconditionally and wants to be in a relationship with you. You can grow to know Him as intimately as you know your daughter. As far as I'm concerned, that beats religion hands down."

Toby went on for some time about God's love and how to receive it. Then they prayed together. By the time Judy left the church, that love Toby had kept talking about had become reality for her, and she walked away much lighter than she could remember ever feeling.

Chapter Eleven

I've been noticing that a lot of the children in the neighborhood come home alone and let themselves into the house with a key they wear on a shoestring around their necks. That really scares me. Some of them are too young to be home alone. I know most of their mothers and know that they can't afford after-school childcare. So what to do? I'm not about to call any authority—these are good mamas for the most part.

Relational goal: Initiate "Neighborhood After-School Study Program." Talk to all the young mothers about having their children come to my house on Mondays and Wednesdays for tutoring until their parents get home. I'll get the Bunko girls to bake cookies for us and volunteer to help with crowd control. This one will hurt. I am used to my peace and quiet, and that many kids will make a racket. But I reckon it will be peaceful in heaven soon enough, so for now I better do what I can to make a difference in their lives. And right after NASP, I'll take an N-A-P.

—FROM EMMA'S JOURNAL, SEPTEMBER 15, 1992

Within two weeks of his own transformation, Ben began another habit after Sunshine went to bed. Instead of sneaking out to the liquor store, he began slipping into his garage where the tools from his former life as a sculptor had lain dormant since

Linda died. Half-formed clay models that no longer brought satisfaction went out with the trash. A flawed chunk of granite went out in the flower bed. He bought several new blocks of wax and began dabbling. He let go of his former, more abstract style and began to shape images that captured memories.

On his turntable, a new form was slowly taking shape. A photo of Linda lay next to it. It was taken on a beach trip—before Sunshine came, before Linda got sick. Ben picked up the photo and looked at it for some time, as he did every evening. Against the backdrop of a blue beach towel, Linda was leaning back on her elbows, her head thrown back in laughter, white teeth flashing, blond hair caught in motion. It was the one picture that Ben had always felt best captured the heat and spirit of the woman he had loved so well for so long. It spoke to him of pure happiness and created in him a longing for that which had been so fleeting in his own life.

Working the wax again brought Ben a peace that no amount of beer had been able to induce. Though it had not been one of his initial goals, after that first night with the clay, he had written in his "Living on Purpose" journal, "I believe I was created to create. Sculpting is what I do best. For me not to sculpt is to deny what God put in me. So my new goal is to go out to the studio at least four nights a week and begin working again."

One late afternoon when he got home from work, Sunshine had a friend with her. This was the first time she had ever brought someone to their home. "Dad, this is Ashley. Ash, my dad, Big Ben." Ashley was initially intimidated by the man's size and hairy exterior. But his big smile and the warm crinkles around his eyes soon calmed her concern. The two girls worked on homework and giggled about boys until Ashley's mom came by to pick her up.

Judy got off work and drove to the address Ashley had given her. As she pulled up to the house, with its torn window screens and its need of paint, she knew it would have been better if she had insisted the girls come to her house to study. When the six-foot-six-inch, bearded giant answered the door, her first impulse was to run. But just as her daughter had, she warmed to the man when he smiled and welcomed her into the tiny living room. "The girls are in the back. I'll let them know you are here."

As Ben walked down the short hall, he regretted that he had procrastinated about taking his shower. He lifted an arm for a quick sniff. His suspicions were confirmed. *Figures. First time in years a nice lady has come by, and I stink.* He tried to suck in his substantial stomach as he reentered the room.

Coincidentally, for the first time in more than a decade, Judy felt herself concerned about how she looked to a man. *Weird. He's sure not the kind of man I'm usually attracted to.* She wished she had taken time that morning to put on at least a little foundation and blush and self-consciously brushed her hair back from her face. That simple gesture brought Ben a twinge of memory, for it was a habit that reminded him of Linda.

Ben and Judy made small talk while waiting for the girls. Judy declined his offer of a cold drink, nervous without really knowing why. Ben asked where she worked, and she told him a little about the post office. She returned the question. When he said he drove a truck for Helping Hands Ministries, her heart jumped.

"The thrift shop on Berry Road? Do you remember picking up a whole houseful of things on Longfellow Street a few weeks ago? Would that have been you?"

It was Ben's turn to be shocked. Emma's journal lay in plain sight, not three feet from where Judy sat. *Do I lie or not?* "Sure I remember. That was the day I fell off the ramp and almost busted my…tail."

Then she asked about it. He knew she was going to, and yet when she did, he panicked.

"What's the big deal about that stupid journal?" he bellowed. "My boss was all over my back about it. Why does everyone seem to think I'm a thief?" Realizing immediately how inappropriate his tone was, he tried to calm down. "I'm sorry. You ought to be talking to the woman who was there that day. She had us load three boxes of stuff in her trunk. If you ask me, that's where you'll find Emma's book."

Judy's blush of interest instantly faded at Ben's angry outburst. Ashley and Sunny walked into the room about that time, both sensing the coolness that had not been there a moment earlier. No one noticed the worn leather journal beside Ben's chair. It was only after she was almost home that Judy wondered how Ben had known her mother's name.

Stu locked his car and walked up the steps to his efficiency apartment. It had been more than a week since he had walked out. Marilyn had tried to call him this morning at the actuarial research firm where he was a partner. He had told his assistant to tell her he was in a meeting. He had not yet returned the phone call, and he wasn't sure he would.

Stu was a creature of habit and had quickly adopted a new routine. Home by six, he would change into running gear, then go out for a run. His slight build hinted at an aptitude for running long distances, and when he would return to the apartment almost an hour later, it was as if the stress of the day had been sweated away. A light dinner of fruit and yogurt, a shower, then a tall glass of iced tea, his favorite chair (the only piece of furniture he'd taken from home), and a biography from some great figure in history. He would read until 9:50, brush his teeth, and be in bed and sound asleep within minutes.

His biggest surprise in leaving Marilyn was the peace he felt. He was sleeping better than ever. His job performance had improved because he was able to give more attention to the business at hand, with no thought wasted on what he would need to do that day to keep peace at home.

Before he finally left her, he had usually escaped to his "ham shack" in the basement as quickly as possible. Now his ham radio gear sat in boxes in a corner, still not hooked up. Every time he saw it, Stu thought about it and wondered how he could set up a radio tower in the apartment complex. But tonight he realized that he didn't miss the hobby a bit. *Guess it was just a way to escape Marilyn's ranting and raving. Might as well sell it and do something with the money.*

He laid down his book and looked at his watch. A little after nine. He picked up the phone, took a deep breath, and pecked in the number. After three rings, she answered.

"Hi, Sis. It's me. Stu. Can we talk for a few minutes?"

Barry Lamb sat in his office, wondering how he had ever gotten to this place. He had always been the good son, the good student, the good pastor. Now he was falling in love with a woman who wasn't his wife. It was worse than that. He was in love (or lust) with a woman he wasn't even sure he liked very much. She had been the chairman of the pastor search committee that had brought him to Overland Park. She had made sure his office was redecorated to his tastes. She sat on the personnel committee and made the recommendation that he receive a nice raise every year. She bragged on his preaching and his appearance. But by now he knew her acts of service were always based on the expectation that sooner or later she would need him and he'd better come running when she called.

Barry had never been a strong man. He loved books, he loved preaching, he loved pastoring. But he was never going to be the kind of pastor who grew a large church. She validated his ministry and made him feel it was noble to pastor a small church. He knew now she liked the church small, the better to keep control.

He looked at the pictures on his desk of his wife and of his grown daughter with her husband and their son. What he was doing was lunacy. It would destroy them if they knew.

He tried to figure out how he had become vulnerable to her advances. She was an attractive woman but not beautiful. She was smart but cold. He supposed that it was her ability to play his emotions like a harp that allowed her to control him. She knew just how to build him up, to stroke his ego, to make him feel like a man. She sent him notes, made calls during the day, just to pass along a compliment. Then it became more personal. An innuendo, a wink, a gentle stroking of his arm while she held his hand after service instead of shaking it. He had never in his life had a woman express that kind of attention to him, not even his wife when they were dating, and it triggered some unmet need deep inside. He was hungry, and Marilyn knew it.

And she could use him. Like the day her mother-in-law had died and she demanded he miss his grandson's third birthday party to come to the hospital.

Now she wanted them to leave together. He was at once terrified and excited by the prospect. Where would they go? How would they live?

His secretary knocked on the door. "Pastor, I'm leaving now. Hey, you want the light on? It's getting dark in here."

"No, thanks," he said. "I've only got a few things to finish up. You go on." Barry sat in the darkness awhile longer, trying to figure out how he was going to get out of this mess. His heart raced, and his hands were shaking.

Graystone Chapel was already full that Sunday before Thanksgiving. Judy and Ashley were there for the seventh week in a row. Week by week Judy grew more comfortable, amazed at how her life seemed to become less complicated and more joyful. Toby's preaching was a big part of that. After every Sunday's message she asked herself, *Why didn't I know this before? I had no idea the Bible had anything to do with real life.*

The worship had already begun. Judy was focused on a song that had become one of her favorites, a song about hope. *Hope* was the word that best described her attitude these days. To her right, Stu stood beside her, worshiping with his eyes closed and his hands raised in the air, a freedom he had never known in Marilyn's church. Stu was awakening more and more every day to the self he had squelched for years. Part of that awakening was spiritual. Between Marilyn and her church, he had just about sworn off God. But now he was finding something that scratched deep down where he itched.

They had been separated now for several weeks. Marilyn's self-imposed standard of righteousness prevented her from filing for divorce; Stu felt no compulsion to do so and was comfortable living in that twilight state of separation.

Ashley elbowed her mother to scoot down the pew and let in some late arrivers on their left. Judy heard her daughter's animated voice and turned to see Ben and Sunshine seated next to them. Her heart quickening again, she turned back to face the front just before having to make eye contact with Ben.

Though the girls still got together frequently, she and Ben had avoided talking ever since that awkward first meeting at his house. The girls now met at Ashley's, and Judy would drop Sunny off in the driveway at her home.

Judy would have preferred that Ashley not even spend time with Sunshine, but her daughter had made so few friends she could not deny her this one. Besides, she had discovered that Sunny was a delightful girl and fun to have around—bright, polite, with a razor sharp sense of humor. She could mimic anyone, from television personalities to teachers and other students. She made Judy laugh even when she didn't know the person she was impersonating.

Sunny had told Ashley that her dad was dragging her to a different church every Sunday, searching for who knows what. Most made them both wonder if they'd ever find God in a church building. Judy overheard and smiled as she thought about the reaction of most congregations when a bearded, ponytailed giant wearing bib overalls walked into their midst.

Ashley was the one who had told Sunny about Graystone Chapel, and now they were actually here. His presence certainly didn't attract any attention; this unique fellowship was used to people who felt free to express themselves creatively in dress and appearance. Judy hated to admit that she felt more than a bit uncomfortable, wondering if Ben's presence would ruin the peace she felt in this sanctuary.

Toby's sermon today was, naturally, on being thankful. Judy had met with Toby several times, and one of the things he had suggested to her was to keep a running list of things she was grateful for. Funny how this simple discipline had helped her keep a better perspective.

Ben sat on the end of the pew, torn between conflicting emotions. On the one hand, this little church, packed with as diverse a crowd of people as he had ever seen, was exactly what he had been hoping for but had almost given up hope of finding. During one song Ben watched in awe as a potter shaped a lump of clay on a wheel, while the congregation sang a song about the potter's hands. The imagery was that of God shaping and molding our lives. Tears streamed down his face into his beard. It was as if he had finally discovered someone who spoke his heart language—the language of the artist.

Yet Judy's presence three bodies down the row made him ill at ease, because he knew his presence made *her* uncomfortable. Every time he had seen her pull into the driveway to bring Sunshine home, he had considered returning her mother's journal to her. But it had become his security blanket, and he dared not let it go. His new life was too fragile, too unstable to risk losing it. That indecision about returning the journal also kept him from apologizing about his outburst that day. Maybe he could say something now, here at church. Surely there was no place better for apologizing.

Toby concluded his talk, and people began gathering their things. Toby asked them to sit tight for a moment while the chairman of the church's missions committee spoke to them briefly.

The news the lanky man in the denim shirt and brown corduroys brought surprised only the people seated on the pew around Judy. Everyone else had already heard it. Seems the church's board of elders had voted to join with the efforts of Emma Estes's neighbors and were trying to purchase her home. When the man with the microphone revealed the plans for the home, both Judy and Stu felt themselves flush first with confusion, then with shame. Did this have something to do with their father's abusive nature?

The congregation greeted the news with applause. Toby came back to the platform and announced that if anyone wanted to give to the purchase of the home, they should make sure the contribution was clearly marked "Emma's House." Dozens of people reached for one of the offering envelopes in the racks on the backs of each pew as they were dismissed.

Neither Judy nor Ben was particularly adept at casual social interchange, so the next few minutes were awkward. Ben congratulated her on the news about her mother's house. Judy said it was all a surprise to her as well, that she didn't know anything about it. Stu stood there quietly, and Judy introduced him. He shook hands with Ben, kissed his sister, and told her he needed to leave, then slipped out.

Skeeter Wilson came in from her tour of duty in preschool ministry, stopping to receive a whispered message from someone as she looked at Judy and Ashley across the room. She quickly made her way to them and gathered both in her arms. "Well, so much for our little surprise," she told them. "I was hoping we'd have the house bought before we told you about what we wanted to do to honor your mother."

"Well, I don't quite know what to say. This really is a surprise. What made you think of it?"

Skeeter was surprised that she asked. "Well, it was Emma's idea. It just seemed that, of all the things your mother cared about, this was the one thing that would best continue the spirit of concern she had for people in bad situations." Skeeter saw something hurting in Judy's eyes. "It's what she wanted. Does it upset you?"

"Oh no. Well, yes. It's just that it hits a little close to home. I don't know how much Mom told you about my father, but he was, well, he was sort of…"

"Told me? Of course she told me. One of Emma's sayings was that 'a secret loses its power over you once it's out in the open, so you might as well let your own secrets out of the bag before someone else does.'"

Skeeter continued to try to read Judy's face. "But you still won't talk about it, will you, honey?"

Judy started to cry, and Skeeter hugged her tight again. Ben had been hanging around and had just about worked up his nerve to apologize for being rude and maybe even bring up the journal. But at the sight of tears, he was out of there.

Ashley stood back, unsure what her mother was experiencing. She waved good-bye to Sunshine and watched her and Ben walk away. Just like most Sundays these days, mother and daughter ended up at Skeeter's and Danny's for lunch, and Judy was able to unpack a little more of her baggage in the shadow of her mother's old home.

Chapter Twelve

I am exhausted. Too much output, not enough input.

Physical goal: Get more sleep.

—FROM EMMA'S JOURNAL, JANUARY 1, 1984

Sunshine was sprawled on the floor of Ashley's bedroom, drilling her friend with Spanish vocabulary words. She came home with Ashley nearly every weekday, and the two girls made good use of their time while their parents were still at work.

Somewhere between *el baile* and *la biblioteca*, Sunshine rolled over to her other side. She noticed two books under Ashley's bed. Reaching to get them, she asked, "Hey, Ash, what are these?"

Ashley was lying on her back on her bed and turned over to see what Sunny was talking about. Too quickly she grabbed them. "Those are personal."

"I just asked what they were. You don't have to freak out and everything."

"Sorry. It's just that this was my grandmother's Bible. See how worn out it is? She read it every day for the last twenty-five years before she died. And this is my journal. My grandma kept one, and now I do too."

"That's so weird."

"What?"

"My dad? He keeps a journal too. He found this old leather book, and it kind of changed his life, you know? So now he—"

"What kind of old leather book? About this big? Where did he find it? How did he get it?"

"Chill, Ash. Take a breath. He found it on his job and stuff, I guess. It's, like, worn-out leather, red, and about this big." She held her hands inches apart.

"That sounds like my grandmother's journal. I found it at her house, then forgot it. When we went back to get it, my aunt had given away all of Grandma's stuff to Helping Hands. Except Helping Hands didn't have it. We've about given up on finding it."

"No worries. If the one my dad found is your grandma's, once he knows who it belongs to, I'm sure you'll get it back."

Neither of the girls was prepared for Judy's reaction when they told her about their potential discovery. Ashley had never heard her mother use language quite like that before. And Sunshine had never heard anyone use that kind of language about her father.

"But we're not even sure it's the same journal, Mom," Ashley said, trying to help her mother calm down.

"I'm sure my dad would've returned it if he'd known who it belonged to," chimed in Sunny.

Judy tried to regain her composure. "We'll see about that."

The two girls got in the backseat of Judy's rusting Jeep Cherokee and arrived at Ben Shoffner's home in record time.

Ben had just gotten home himself, sore and tired from a long day of pickups but anxious to share some good news with Sunshine—some incredible news with the potential to change their lives forever. He had just opened a soft drink and was contemplating a shower when he heard Judy's car pull into the driveway, as he did most afternoons. Grinning, he opened the door to greet his daughter.

He never saw it coming.

Hurricane Judy hit the door, and the tempest raged. She screamed. She cursed. She even tried to slap and hit the man more than twice her size. Every time he opened his mouth, another storm surge came. He finally quit trying to talk and began backing his way into the living room to his chair. Reaching down without taking his eyes off her, Ben picked up Emma Estes's journal and gave it to Judy. "I'm so sorry," he repeated over and over. "Please let me try to explain," he finally added.

Having the journal in hand released some of the pressure within Judy, but she was still too emotional to try to repair the damage done. She paused only long enough on her way out to tell Sunshine, "Honey, I'm not mad at you. You are still welcome at our house." Then Judy grabbed her daughter's hand and fled in the Jeep, slinging gravel in every direction as they left the Shoffner driveway.

Skeeter sat with the cordless phone on her lap, knowing that just as soon as she hung up from one call, another was coming in. The For Sale sign in Emma's yard was gone, and everyone wanted to know what had happened.

Just last night Shauna Cochran had called to say the total

collected so far came to just over forty thousand dollars. The price had come down to sixty-eight thousand, but they were still a long way from being able to pay cash and avoid a mortgage. Now it looked as if it was too late. Skeeter had called Mr. Sullivan, the Realtor, to ask who had bought it, but he had not returned her phone call. When the phone finally quieted, Skeeter sat and cried.

That evening was too chilly for the neighbors to meet on the Wilsons' porch. The wind had shifted and was now coming from the north, and a few snowflakes were beginning to fall. Though Christmas lights were up in abundance, no one felt any holiday cheer.

Still they came, and Skeeter's tiny living room was soon filled beyond capacity. Several people had brought a snack to share, Danny was making popcorn, and Tom McAllister brought several bottles of his homemade wine to warm their dreary souls.

The room felt like a wake even though there was no casket. But a dream had died, a dream that so many had been sure was from God. They talked about what Emma had called "the coulda, woulda, shouldas," knowing they could never relive the past, yet they were so reluctant to let it go.

The phone rang. "Hello?" Skeeter said above the din. "Hello? Hang on a minute, I can't hear a word." After shushing the crowd, she said, "All right now, who is this? Oh, hello, Pastor. Yes, yes of course. Come right over. Oh, by the way, have you heard about... Pastor? I guess he hung up."

Not sure as to the nature of Toby's visit, Skeeter didn't know whether to send her guests home or not. Before she could make up her mind, the pastor walked in with Judy and Stu Estes beside him.

Skeeter introduced the brother and sister, along with the pastor, to those in the crowd who didn't attend Graystone Chapel. After offering them a snack and something to drink, which they all declined, Skeeter asked, "Do we need to go in the kitchen to talk?"

"Not at all. I came here to tell you something exciting. I didn't realize you had company. But I think what we have to share concerns everyone here, so may I just say a word to everybody?"

"Oh, please do."

"Friends, all of you are aware that Emma's house was taken off the market yesterday. We were all afraid, afraid that our hope of fulfilling Emma's dream had crumbled. This afternoon I got a call from Stu, whom most of you know is Emma's son. We met, and he shared something with me that… Well, you tell 'em, Stu."

Stu paled at being on the spot and deferred to his sister, who also indicated her desire for the pastor to continue. Toby said, "Okay, you two. Now stop me if I don't get this right, okay? I'll do my best."

Turning back to the crowded room, he continued, "A couple of years ago Emma asked that Stu's wife, Marilyn, take care of her affairs. No one knows for sure all the reasons why, and we won't presume to know the motive of either Marilyn or Emma." In spite of his caveat, murmurs rumbled around the room.

"Marilyn had been trying to sell the home, believing that was her responsibility. Without going into all the nitty-gritty details, let me just say that as of four o'clock yesterday afternoon, Emma's will was found…" Without hearing the rest, the crowd cheered, laughed, and whistled. "Her will was found inside her journal…" Another cheer went up. "And in that will, Judy and Stu inherited Emma's home, to do with as they deem best. After discussing the contents of that will with one another and sleeping on it, Stu and Judy are here to announce their intent to *donate* the house to Graystone Chapel in order that we may fulfill Emma's dream for the home."

There was an audible gasp from everyone, then the loudest cheer of the night. People began hugging Stu, shaking his hand, slapping him on his slender back until he almost lost his balance, not to mention his composure. Judy received the same treatment after Skeeter released her from a bear hug. A few went out to share the good news with those neighbors who had been too despondent to go to Skeeter's home initially, and before long they came to join the wake-turned-celebration.

Chapter Thirteen

I was feeling awfully lonely last night. Wishing I had a man to hold hands with, to snuggle with, to keep warm with. Started to feel I was missing out on something, not having a husband anymore. As difficult as Frank was, I loved him. And in spite of his flaws, we had our special times. Can God ever meet those same needs now that Frank is gone? I'd better find out soon because I'm about to go out and marry the first man with a pulse that I meet.

Spiritual goal: To meditate every morning (until I believe) on the love of God, His blessings, and His goodness. He is sufficient for my every need. I know it in my head, and I will focus on it until I know it in my heart.

—FROM EMMA'S JOURNAL, FEBRUARY 14, 1981

I t was a while before the crowd went home, but Pastor Toby had excused himself right after the announcement in order to get home and tuck his young children into bed. Stu and Judy stayed behind because Judy really wanted to let Skeeter in on the rest of the story.

Judy told her of the day they had driven away from Ben's in complete silence after discovering the journal. Ashley, though angry at her mother's behavior, had taken the journal from her mother's hands as soon as they got into the car and had read it while they drove. As they walked in the kitchen, Judy had asked Ashley to let her see it.

Clutching it to her chest, Ashley had begun to sob. "You didn't have to freak out like that, Mom. You embarrassed me in front of my only friend and acted just awful. I was so humiliated I wanted to die. Grandma would never have acted that way." With that, Ashley had flung the journal at her mother before running to her bedroom.

Too tired to confront her, Judy had let her go and picked up the journal, which had fallen with its cover up and pages askew after skidding across the kitchen floor. Almost every page was covered with Emma's fine handwriting. Judy had read the first paragraph, the one Ashley had read to her the previous summer. The words hadn't registered though; she was still so upset by everything—Ben's thievery, her reaction, and now Ashley's mortification—that she couldn't focus on the words. She had turned the book over in her hands, held it to her cheek, and tried to remember what she had thought finding this book would finally resolve.

"Did you answer that question?" asked Skeeter.

"No, still working on it," said Judy.

She had opened it again, she told Skeeter, this time in reverse, looking for the last entry. Just inside the back cover, a tiny corner of fine paper had peeked from behind the binding. Upon closer examination, she had discovered a slit between the book's cover and lining, resealed with rubber cement. Working it loose with her thumbnail, she had pulled from it the paper she had discovered.

She had read just a few lines, enough to recognize what it was, and grabbed the phone to call her brother.

"Stu, what did you think when you heard what your sister had found?" wondered Skeeter.

Stu literally jumped at the sound of his name. He had not told anyone the full details of what had happened next—not Toby, not Judy.

"Well, I was obviously excited that she had found the will but troubled at the implications. My wife had lied to me. There was a bigger breach in our relationship than I had thought. I don't know if Judy told you,"—he looked at his sister—"but Marilyn and I have been separated for a while now. I guess I thought we might eventually get back together, but this, this was something else. So I got in the car and went over to the house to confront Marilyn."

Stu paused. "Could I have a drink of water or something?"

"Of course, dear." Skeeter bounded up from her chair and was back from the kitchen with a full glass in seconds. When Stu took a sip, his hand was shaking.

"When I got there, there was another car in the driveway. I thought I recognized the blue Buick, but I just didn't want to believe it. As I walked to the front door, I could see between the blinds enough to know that the living room was empty. I knocked. No answer. I knocked again, then took a deep breath and used my key to unlock the door." Stu paused and took another sip. His face was the color of his gray suede shoes.

Sensing where this might be going, Skeeter patted his arm and said, "You don't have to tell me this, honey."

"No, it's okay. Well, as I let myself in, I didn't want to jump to conclusions, and I didn't want to startle her either, because she keeps a pistol in her nightstand drawer. So I stood at the bottom of the stairs and called as loud as I could, 'Marilyn, are you home?' There was a lot of noise from our bedroom, and Marilyn came flying out with her dressing gown wrapped tight around her. 'What are you doing here?' she screamed at me. 'Get out! Get out before I call the police!'"

Another sip of water. Stu looked at his shoes, talking to them. "By now I knew what was up. I said, 'I'll get out as soon as we talk about my mother's will. Maybe your pastor would like to come down and hear this as well.' She really flipped then, charging down the stairs as if she was going to kill me. Just as she was about to reach me, the Reverend Lamb appeared in the bedroom doorway, tucking in his shirt. He said, 'Marilyn, leave him alone. It's time the truth came out. I can't live with this another day.'"

This unexpected turn of Stu's story was making Skeeter literally squirm with discomfort. She knew that pastors were not perfect people. She even knew that some fell into immorality—the story was not unfamiliar. But this story was almost too much for her. "I think I need a drink of water myself," she said and got up to buy some time.

Judy chimed in, "Make mine a double." She leaned over on the couch and hugged her brother, something she couldn't remember doing in a long, long time.

As Skeeter emerged from the kitchen, Judy asked, "How could a pastor, of all men, be attracted to someone like Marilyn? She's not unattractive, at least not until you get to know her." She glanced at her brother to make sure she hadn't offended him.

Skeeter thought a moment and said, "It's a funny thing, infatuation. It's not always based on something rational. I've seen young people marry who were head over heels in love but didn't even really appreciate each other as friends. My guess is that the reverend was attracted to her strength, not her beauty. From what I've heard, he sounds a little indecisive to me. Some men seem to need to be told what to do."

"Marilyn was good at that," Stu deadpanned.

After sipping her water, Skeeter took a deep breath and said, "Okay, then what happened?"

"What happened was, in spite of being caught on the brink of adultery, this woman, who was always so condemning of everyone else's sin, remained a defiant bully. But her pastor, Reverend Lamb, was so eaten up with guilt that he cracked. I mean, he really spilled the beans. Marilyn had destroyed the original will, he said, not knowing that Mom had made a copy and placed it in the back of her journal.

"Apparently he and Marilyn have been involved, to some degree, for years," Stu continued. "I guess I should have noticed. He claimed it had never been sexual until that night and that I had come in right before they—well, you know. At first I thought, *Yeah, right.* But now I'm inclined to believe him.

"Seems they had been talking for some time about just disappearing. The only problem was, Marilyn is used to a particular lifestyle. She's accustomed to our making good money, and an adulterous preacher could never have another church, so she had been squirreling money away for some time. She had thought Mom's house would sell quickly, and they'd get the money and finally have enough to take off. The longer the house took to sell, the colder Reverend Lamb's feet got. He actually had come over to the house that very night to call the whole thing off, at least that's what he said. Evidently, Marilyn had taken him upstairs to shut him up and, you might say, seal the deal."

"Did *she* tell you that?" Judy wondered, her tone indicating she was sickened by the thought.

"Oh no. She just sat and stared daggers at me the whole time. Barry Lamb was sobbing and shaking as he told me everything."

"Honey, how are you feeling about all this?" asked Skeeter.

Stu thought a long while before answering. His analytical brain was unaccustomed to probing the potential land mines of feelings. Looking at Judy, he said, "I was sick about it. Then mad...some. I'm surprised I wasn't angrier. I actually felt sorry for Reverend Lamb. If what Toby has been telling us is true, if God wants us to show repentance for our sins, then I think Reverend Lamb's going to be all right with God someday. But Marilyn...even after being *caught in the act,* she's still as self-righteous as ever."

"Honey," said Skeeter, "with her kind, I suspect it's hard to be honest with yourself, let alone the Almighty."

Stu considered that for a moment and nodded. "I think you're right. She's all about control, apparently at any price. She wanted absolute control of that little church...and I guess she got it. Anyway, that's the story. Talk about a soap opera. Who'd have thought such a thing could happen? I just wish I had been smart enough to figure her out years ago."

Skeeter leaned back in her chair and peered at the ceiling for a response. "There's no use wasting energy on that one, Stu. You figured it out now, and that's what matters. The only question now is, What will you do with it?"

"I don't know. As I left, she said she would never file for divorce, that she wouldn't have it on her conscience." Stu chuckled. "Whatever that means. So I guess I'll have to file before she tries to steal something else. But I honestly don't care about the house or the stuff. That was all hers anyway; it was what she thought would make her happy. But she was never happy. Never."

He looked across the room, seeing nothing. "I'm not sure if I still love her or what is the right thing to do. I never in a million years thought I'd even be thinking about divorce. I just figured that Marilyn was a life sentence for something terrible I'd done." He swallowed and looked down at his feet.

"Just don't put off for too long the hard work of forgiving her," Skeeter said. "Forgiveness is not about letting her off the hook; it's getting you off her hook."

Stu nodded. "I can't say I'm ready to do that right now. At the same time, I don't feel like it's going to be impossible. I'm honestly not interested in hurting Reverend Lamb, so any confession to their church will have to come from him, not me. I bet he'll resign next Sunday. Even though he almost committed the ultimate sin in that church's eyes, he's basically a little bug that got caught in the web of a black widow." Slapping his knees and scooting forward on the couch, he changed the tone of the conversation. "Anyway, now that we've got Mom's house, and it can be used for something good, it's all working out for the best."

"Why didn't your mother ever tell anyone else about the will or tell you all about her plans, I wonder?" asked Skeeter.

"Well, it wasn't like she had a chance," said Judy. "As far as we know, she never awakened from the stroke."

"I guess that's right. But I meant earlier. Emma had such discernment about people, I'm just surprised."

"It was her test," said Danny, whose shape took form in the shadow of the hall.

"Why, Danny, have you been eavesdropping?" Skeeter scolded.

"No, I been listenin'."

"What did you say about a test?" asked Judy.

"It was the trust test. Miz Emma told me that sometimes all people needed was to be trusted. So she gave them a test, and she said they usually passed. She trusted me a lot. An' that made me do what was right."

Skeeter pondered this and shrugged her shoulders. "Sounds like Emma, all right. That's the reason so many kids in this neighborhood loved her. They knew she saw them not as they were but as they could be. It makes a difference."

"Yeah, well, in this case, someone flunked the test," said Stu as he stood. "I've got to be going. Big meeting at work in the morning." He reached out to shake hands with Skeeter, who would allow no such thing as she pulled him in for another hug. Judy hugged the two of them at the same time, and they walked out to their cars.

Across town Ben Shoffner kissed his daughter good-night and walked into the little dining room turned studio. Since winter's arrival, it was too cold to work in the garage. He passed a small Christmas tree with a far larger than usual pile of presents underneath it.

After lighting his pipe, Ben removed a plastic sheet from the wax figure of the reclining woman. Long, wavy hair fell from her head as her face froze around a full belly laugh. Ben had captured the laugh lines around her eyes, the ease with which she reclined on her elbows, and the relaxed confidence of a woman who knew no fears or worries.

He spun it slowly, around and around on the large turntable, making sure it was interesting from every angle. He held a small carving tool in hand, trying to decide if he was done. A few touches here and there, a slight reworking of one earlobe, then it came— that emotional release that whispered to his soul, *It's finished.*

He walked over to get his journal and poured a cup of decaf coffee, then went back in front of the sculpture and sat down. He opened the rapidly filling spiral notebook to the next blank page and began to write.

Who'd have thought that in four months I would change from a depressed drunk to...whoever, whatever I am today? Tonight I've just completed the sculpture of Linda, which I call "Forever Joy."

Three weeks ago I ran into an old artist friend who is now running a foundation. He'd been asked to commission a sculptor to create the centerpiece for the lobby of some corporation's headquarters. He asked if I was still sculpting, and I was able to tell him I was. He described what they were looking for, and I submitted a few sketches and a rough model.

Just a few days ago I found out I got the commission. The advance on this piece was more money than I've made in any one year of my life. I quit my job driving for Helping Hands to sculpt full-time. With part of the advance, I'm giving Sunny the best Christmas she's ever known. And for myself, I'm going to cast "Forever Joy" in bronze. This piece is for me. It captures the essence of the woman who loved me so well and whose absence grieves me still.

He put down his pen and gave his coffee a slurp. He brought back the image of his daughter reclining in her bed as he had kissed her good night. While they talked, she had struck a pose similar to the one before him now, and his eyes had watered. He began to write again.

While Linda is now absent, Sunshine is very much present. I am grateful to God for the way He has preserved her gentle spirit in spite of my many shortcomings. And I am especially grateful for Emma Estes, whose example pulled me out of my pit and gave me a reason to hope again.

Another sip of coffee and a final sentence.

Lord, in spite of all the good that's come from the journal, I'm still ashamed about how I got it in the first place. Please help Judy Estes to forgive me, and help me forgive myself.

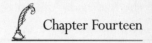

Chapter Fourteen

Gardening is getting so difficult, but I really love working in the
yard. If only my knees would hold up. Skeeter keeps trying to get me
to use her brother, Danny, but he's so slow. I hate to even write this
down, but he just aggravates me. I'm never mean to him or
anything, but I sure don't go out of my way to befriend him. And
yet I sense You telling me to love him, Lord, and build him up. It
will be difficult, but I will.

Relational goal: Teach Danny how to separate the daylilies and
bury the bulbs so the squirrels don't get them. And shower him with
love and cookies the whole while.

—FROM EMMA'S JOURNAL, JUNE 16, 1998

A few weeks later Judy Estes kissed her daughter good night and
sat down with her own little leather-bound book of mostly
blank pages.

In the time since she had recovered her mother's journal, her
life had started to blossom after a long, cold winter of many years.
The emotional and spiritual healing that had begun in Toby's office
that day had really picked up momentum since she'd begun the
habit of the "Living on Purpose" journal.

The day after she and Stu had met with Skeeter, Judy had come
home from work with Ashley's favorite pizza. "We need to talk,"

she had said. And talk they did, for several hours. Judy had told Ashley how sorry she was for embarrassing her at the Shoffners' that day and had encouraged Ashley to have Sunshine over again.

Ashley had been unresponsive at first, but she had finally broken the silence by asking her mother if she planned on forgiving Ben. "I don't think I can bear to face Sunshine until you take back the nasty things you said about her dad."

Judy hadn't been able to make that promise but had said she'd pray about it. Later she had laughed about how much her life had changed. Just a few months ago those would have been the last words to ever come out of her mouth. But she had resolved things with her daughter, and from that day there had been a new dimension in their relationship. Each evening mother and daughter had read each other excerpts from Emma's journal. Most entries summarized a goal that had been responsible for making her the woman she had felt God calling her to become. Each one gave them greater insights into the mother and grandmother they had missed knowing.

This evening they had read an entry from January 17, 1984. It was Emma's sixtieth birthday, therefore a longer entry than usual.

> *Today I'm reminded again of the brevity of life and the difficulty of change. The first we are not always aware of. The second we cannot forget. I'm convinced there lies within each heart the need to make our lives count. When this need is realized, I believe we have*

discovered the secret to happiness. We grow confused and think that our lives will count if we achieve some measure of fame or wealth or power. In reality, all these things we chase after create more hunger than satisfaction. For me, investing in the lives of others has brought a satisfaction that lingers without end.

I now begin my seventh decade of life. How quickly the first six have passed. How much time I wasted, drifting along, never believing that one day I would be what many consider an old woman. If only I had begun the effort to live on purpose as a young woman. I could have made a difference in the lives of Judy and Stu. I could have found the courage to make a safe and peaceful home for them, regardless of the cost. I could have—well, I could have done many things. I've been down this path too many times. The one thing I've learned is the futility of the woulda, coulda, shouldas. I cannot change the past, but I can take steps toward a better future.

This year, my sixty-first year on earth, I begin with the following goals, and when at some point in the year they become habits or cease to stretch me, I will set new ones.

Intellectual: I'm always intrigued when I see quotes by C. S. Lewis. This year I will read everything I can find by him and see if there's a course about him at the community college.

Physical: This past year I lost ground in the ongoing battle to eat better. This year I will keep it even simpler than usual. Eat more vegetables. Every day. That's it. I'll try new kinds, find new ways to cook them. I refuse to let an undisciplined diet rob me of health and vigor in my remaining years.

Spiritual: If I am to continue to be the kind of friend that I *want to be to my neighbors and church family, I must do better at regularly scheduling time alone for silence and solitude. In addition to giving God the first hour of every day, on Tuesday afternoons I will not answer the phone or the door. I will let everyone know I am unavailable during that time in order that I may be long alone with my heavenly Father. If I cannot sit at His feet and hear His voice and know His will, then everything else I do will be in vain.*

Relational: Wanda Dawson just had a little baby boy. His name is Clarence. He'll have no father to guide him, and Wanda must work to support him. So, Lord, if You will help me, I'm going to be little Clarence's surrogate grandmother. I'll love him as if he were my own flesh and blood. I'll read him the stories of the faith. I'll invest in his education, volunteering in his classroom when he starts school. I cannot make a difference with every little boy who is born into this world without a daddy, but I can make a difference with this one. Lord, help me make a difference in Clarence Dawson's life.

Judy thumbed through the worn pages one more time before picking up her own journal again. She opened it to the first page and reread those words copied from her mother's own hand.

Unwilling to live my life in the future the way I've lived it in the past, I resolve that—submitted to God and with His help—I will become each day more like the person He created me to be.

Four simple goals were already becoming habits for her. Her intellectual goal was to learn about investing, and she had already read two books on the subject of financial freedom. These had the effect of fueling her dreams of life after the post office. Her physical goal of walking every day was helping her keep the binging of the holiday season under control. Ashley walked with her most mornings before school, even in the dark and the cold, inspired by her grandmother's passion for walking. Judy's spiritual goal was to read one of the psalms each evening before bedtime. These ancient prayers were helping her to see that there was much more to prayer than "Now I lay me down to sleep…" Her relational goal had been the hardest—to find a friend with whom she could unload the rest of her secrets. Skeeter's words continued to echo in her mind.

At first Judy couldn't imagine who that friend would be. But it soon became clear that her mother's closest friend, Skeeter Wilson, was more than willing to fill the role of the friend, the mentor—of the mother she grieved over not knowing.

Judy relished these seeds of change taking hold in her life. She had just glanced at the old clock on the mantel and was thinking about getting ready for bed when the phone rang. It was Stu. He now called several times a week around this time. Often there was no agenda, just the natural touching of hearts that they had known so little of. But this night, she sensed something bubbling under the surface. He needed no prompting to tell her about it.

"I saw Marilyn today."

"What! What for?"

"I called and asked her to go to lunch. She thought I was there to serve her with divorce papers. I let her sweat it all through lunch.

Finally I said, 'Marilyn, my dad was an abusive man. He was always screaming at Mom, Judy, and me. We were never good enough for him. He found fault with everything we did. I grew up feeling like I was a failure.'

"Then I said, 'When we got married, it was the happiest day of my life. I thought I must really be someone if I could find a woman as pretty as you.'"

"In other words, you lied to her."

"No, I wasn't lying. I really thought she was pretty—when we first met, I mean. Anyway I said, 'Marilyn, I married someone just like my daddy. I was never good enough for him to love me, and I've never been good enough for you. And I probably never will be. But, Marilyn, I just want you to know that I forgive you, not only for what you did with Reverend Lamb, but for all those years of being so controlling. I forgive you.'"

There was silence as Judy waited for him to finish. "And?"

"And she started crying."

"No way!"

"I'm serious. Her eyes got red, then the tears just puddled out of her eyes. It was the first time in all these years that I've ever seen her shed a real tear. I was shocked."

"So am I. What did she say?"

"She didn't say a word. Just reached across the table, squeezed my hand, and walked out."

"Oh man! I can't believe she didn't say anything."

"But she did. The tears, that squeeze. There was a bigger message in that than in any words she'd ever said."

"But you're still divorcing her, right?" There was a long pause. "Stu?"

"I don't know yet. I guess I want to believe she'll soften up some. Don't think I'm weird, but I've really been praying for her. I think if God could do the miracles in the Bible, if He can change lives like some of those at Graystone Chapel, maybe He can change her, heal her. Just look at what's He's doing in my life. I may not have been as obvious as Marilyn, but I share plenty of responsibility for our marriage not working."

"Well, don't let me burst your bubble, but I'd say that Marilyn's religion has inoculated her against God's healing touch. Forgive me if this hurts you, but I really hope you get rid of her for good."

"I know. But I'm willing to give her another shot if there's a real change in her. If I do, I hope you'll give her a shot as well."

The phrase sent a word picture through Judy's mind, but she kept it to herself.

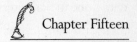

Chapter Fifteen

I wish I had the time and energy to paint, sculpt, or do some
kind of creative thing. About all I've done has been handwork. I
went through the counted cross-stitch phase, my quilting phase, and
the knitting phase. I lost interest in all of them after a while. God
gave me an eye for beautiful things but evidently not the hand to
create them. I just don't have the time to give to learning
something new, so I'll have to settle for appreciating beauty
wherever I see it.

Intellectual goal: Spend a day a month at the Nelson Art
Gallery downtown. I'll take a few of the kids and make a field trip
out of it.

—FROM EMMA'S JOURNAL, AUGUST 23, 1996

The spring crocus, daffodils, and grape hyacinth had already come and gone, and the summer peonies had bloomed and fallen in front of the house that had belonged to Emma Estes. The hollyhocks were at the height of their glory, the most visible evidence that someone had been spending a lot of time and energy in the August heat making sure the flower beds were well cared for. The grass was mowed and trimmed; the old gravel driveway had been paved.

The exterior of the house had a fresh coat of white paint, the trim done in dark green. Every window sparkled, and the brass kick plate and handles on the front door had been polished to a high sheen. A banner hung across the front porch proclaiming this to be "Emma's House: A Place to Begin Again," and at least a hundred balloons were tethered to its posts.

Behind the house the once huge backyard had been made much smaller—a portion of the yard having been paved over to make a parking lot, one that was invisible from the street. A large addition built on to the back of the house blended in well, looking as if it had been constructed that way from the beginning.

The remaining portion of the yard had some new shrubbery that would grow to become a privacy hedge around a beautiful, secluded sanctuary. A small pond gurgled peacefully, while Japanese koi swam undisturbed. Something sat behind the pond, covered with a sheet. On the other side, away from the driveway and protected by a discreet but secure fence, was a playground full of intriguing possibilities for future young residents.

Inside, the transformation was even more remarkable. The tiny living room and dining room had been opened up to create one large, multipurpose room where the residents could take meals and watch television. The two downstairs bedrooms were now linked so that a mother could have some privacy while still having instant access to her children.

The kitchen had also been expanded to accommodate more people, one wall bumped out to provide room for a walk-in pantry, commercial refrigerator, and freezer.

In the back, three rooms similar to the one downstairs awaited mothers with children, while two more bedrooms with private baths were ready for women who came to this haven alone.

The old back porch was now a small office by day and a place for security to keep watch by night. A sun porch now extended off the east side, where four brand-new computers waited for someone to come learn the skills that would open up employment opportunities.

The crowd began gathering at noon, although the festivities didn't start until one o'clock. People of every color and every socio-economic level mingled. A year ago they had gathered for Emma's funeral. Today they were united by their efforts to make Emma's dream a reality. Tables had been set up earlier and were now being covered with foods of all kinds, including Danny's ribs, hot dogs, tamales, kimchi, and homemade peach ice cream.

The final total received by the neighborhood coalition had been just enough to pay for the materials to remodel and cover the addition in back. Not one dime had to be spent on labor, because so many of the neighbors were in the building trades.

Graystone Chapel had included basic operating expenses for Emma's House in their annual budget, so this dream was well on its way to becoming self-sufficient. Pastor Toby had arrived early with his wife, Tina, and their three preschoolers. He stood by the playground where he could watch the kids play and was laughing at one of Oscar Fuentes's stories. Skeeter was close to achieving her goal of hugging every single person in attendance. Shauna Cochran had a small table set up on the front porch, and a steady stream of people were making pledges toward the ongoing expenses of Emma's House.

A crowd of people wanting to visit surrounded Judy and Ashley. And a block down the street Stu and Marilyn sat in his Audi.

"Are you ready to go join the festivities?" Stu asked. Marilyn just shook her head. "I'll wait until you're ready," he told her.

At one o'clock someone fired up the sound system borrowed from the church, and Toby stood, repeated one of Oscar's jokes, then gave thanks for the meal. Everyone got busy, and within thirty minutes the tables once bowed with food were beginning to look sparse.

Danny Wilson had been the one responsible for getting the grounds in such beautiful shape. Now he and Lady patrolled the perimeter, on the lookout for any trash that didn't quite find the receptacles.

Shortly after two, Toby, the de facto master of ceremonies, took the microphone again and quickly introduced the real force behind this day, Skeeter Wilson. Skeeter made the appropriate show of not wanting to be in front of the crowd but quickly displayed the leadership skills that had led to this day.

After giving thanks to a long list of people for making the day possible, she pulled out her notes and set her reading glasses on her nose.

"We are here today to witness a miracle. The miracle is not this house, although that is miracle enough in itself. Here women and children who have been abused and hurt will find a safe shelter and a place to heal, to grow, and to dream again. That is the vision that inspired so many of you to give of your money, your time, and your energy.

"But I believe we are witnessing a bigger miracle today. That miracle is the result of one life, lived on purpose, which in turn has impacted so many others. This house began as a dream of one woman, who herself had experienced the fear and pain of abuse. That woman was our friend, Emma Estes."

At the mention of that name, the crowd began clapping, then cheering. Those who had been seated stood. As one, they remembered the petite woman with the big heart who had invested in each of their lives, and those memories made them applaud all the harder. Stu stood with Marilyn, and Judy and Ashley stood as well, their faces streaming with tears.

Skeeter held up a hand, looking for all the world like one who spoke in public every day. When the crowd had quieted, she continued, "I moved across the street from Emma Estes in 1976, just a few months after her husband had died. She was shy, unsure of herself, and going through the change of life." To the nervous laughter of the crowd, she expressed surprise. "Well, she was. As the years went by—and believe me, they go by faster every year—we became good friends.

"I've never seen someone change so much over time, and change for the better. She lost weight. She learned Spanish. She was the first on the block to own a computer and have e-mail. She subscribed to more magazines about more different subjects than anyone else I know. Every kid in town knew to come to Miss Emma's when a school project was due; she knew more about more things than anyone around. Besides that, there was always food at Miss Emma's house." The collective memory kicked off another laugh from the crowd.

"Em became the neighborhood expert on gardening. She taught who knows how many of us how to keep a budget. She taught our kids in Sunday school and taught a lot of us old ladies how to pray.

"The year her husband died she made two decisions that I believe were responsible for changing the course of her life. First, she decided to become a follower of Jesus Christ. That led her to a study of the Bible, where she was hit over the head by an overlooked little verse in Luke's gospel: chapter 2, verse 52. 'And Jesus grew in wisdom and stature, and in favor with God and men.'

"That's how she began keeping her 'Living on Purpose' journal. How many of you here are now keeping a 'Living on Purpose' journal?" Two-thirds of the crowd raised their hands.

"Isn't it amazing how that little record of simple goals in four areas of life can make such a difference? Emma always said that most people try to change too much at one time, and that's why they grow discouraged and quit. She taught us to take life like the guy who had to eat the elephant, one bite at a time." The crowd chuckled at the memory of one of Emma's time-worn aphorisms.

"I always thought I was Emma Estes's best friend. Later I found out that *everyone* who knew Emma thought they were her best friend. That's what made her so special.

"Emma had a real heart for the ones other people avoided or paid no attention to. People of different colors or those who talked funny. Young people with odd clothes or tattoos or doodads poked through their ears and noses." A twenty-something man with multiple tattoos and a hair color not found in nature stood and took a bow as the crowd laughed yet again.

"Mostly she worried about those who had no one to look after them. Those who were hurt by others, without a defender. Not long before the Lord took her home, she began to talk to different ones of us about a dream of starting a safe house for battered women. Today Emma's dream is a reality, because as she grew herself, she invested herself in so many of us. We are now entrusted with the same spirit of becoming all God created us to be. We are the recipients of her love; let us now be conduits of love to others."

The crowd was wild in its enthusiasm, clapping and cheering as if the Kansas City Royals had just won the World Series.

"At this time I'd like to introduce you to the woman who has been asked to serve as the director of Emma's House. I first met her at Emma's funeral, almost a year ago today. She and her daughter started attending Graystone Chapel, and soon thereafter she became my friend. I'm proud to now turn the microphone over to Emma's daughter, Judy Estes."

As the slender woman with the short haircut and the bright spring dress took the platform, several heads went together, asking if this was really the same daughter they had met those long months ago. Could she have changed so much?

"Thank you, Skeeter, for the nice things you said about my mother. Many of you know that Stu and I had not been close to our mother since we left home, and we say that to our shame and our loss. I hope that each of you will learn a lesson from our mistake and get reacquainted with your own parents if they are still living. Once they are gone, you won't have that opportunity."

While some in the crowd marveled at her poise, none was more surprised than Judy herself. She had joined Toastmasters just a month earlier, right after she took early retirement from the post office. She had done so because of something her mother had written: "Identify your biggest fear, then identify a way to defeat it."

"I have discovered a great deal about myself over the past four or five months. Some I learned from Mom's journal, some from Skeeter, some from my brother, Stu." Stu smiled back at her. Marilyn continued to look at the ground.

"One of the things I discovered was how much I allowed the things of the past to continue to affect my present and my future. As Skeeter mentioned, our own family knew something of abuse, and I did not know how to handle the pain and confusion that resulted from that. I didn't know how to live life on purpose. I just kind of floated along with the current, not realizing I could paddle.

"A month ago I retired after thirty-one years with the post office. I am now just about the same age my mother was when she began to experience intentional growth and change in her own life. My hope is that through the ministry of this place, my life can have just a fraction of the impact my mother's had. Thank you."

Skeeter came back up beside her and hugged her tight. She motioned for Ashley, Stu, and Marilyn to come forward. Marilyn declined, but Stu and Ashley came up hand in hand. In recent months, Stu had grown close to his niece. The two even resembled each other, to the point that more than one onlooker thought they were father and daughter.

When Stu had moved back in with Marilyn, one of his conditions was that she never again talk about Judy or Ashley in derogatory tones. She had kept her word. Even Judy had to admit that her ugly spirit had dissipated quite a bit since her encounter with true forgiveness.

Skeeter took the microphone in one hand, a large scrapbook in the other. "Kids, this is a little something we came up with to help you in some way get better acquainted with the Emma that we all knew and loved. We asked everyone who had been touched by her to write a letter telling a little bit about how Emma had made a difference in their lives. I've had the chance to leaf through it, and take it from me, you'll need a box of tissues handy when you read it!"

Son, daughter, and granddaughter received it, along with another round of hugs before stepping down. Skeeter waited for the applause to stop, then said, "Finally we get to the last part of our festivities today. There was someone else who didn't get to know Emma in life but who was deeply affected by her just from reading her journal. His name is Ben Shoffner. He's here today with his beautiful daughter, Sunshine."

Ben had on a tie, perhaps for the first time in his life. He had lost some of his stomach, but he still looked like Goliath as he and Sunshine approached the platform. Skeeter briefly told the story of how Ben had ended up with the journal and what it had done in his life. Judy tried to keep her face relaxed, but her stomach was churning.

Skeeter continued, "I tried to get Ben to tell it himself, but he's a shy one. We'll work on him, won't we, folks? Anyway, Ben here is a sculptor. He had not created anything in a long time, ever since his wife, Linda, had died of cancer. But reading Emma's journal inspired him to start keeping one of his own, and one of the many wonderful things that happened was that he started sculpting again.

"When he found out about Emma's House, he caught me after church and told me what he had in mind to do to participate. I thought it was a great idea, and so did Pastor Toby. We wanted to keep it a surprise to as many people as possible, so that's why we didn't let everyone know."

As she said this, Skeeter was looking at Judy, who was decidedly uncomfortable. "Clarence? Where's Clarence? Okay, honey, would you please unveil the statue in the garden? And now, ladies and gentlemen, if you'll move around to the back of the house with me, you'll see Ben's tribute to his wife, Linda, a beautiful piece called *Forever Joy.* It is my prayer that this becomes the pose of every woman who visits Emma's House. Thank you for coming."

With that, the crowd quickly moved to the back of the house. More than a few reached for tissues and began dabbing at their eyes when they saw the beautiful bronze piece. It looked as though the woman had just flopped on her back to rest in the grass beside the garden pond, without a care in the world. There was something about her posture, raised up on her elbows, head thrown back in laughter, that struck a chord of hope.

As Emma's family came around the back of the house, Ashley

ran ahead to hug Sunshine. The two girls still stayed in touch at school but hadn't been in each other's home since the night Judy had retrieved the journal. Ben was standing there receiving compliments, feeling both uncomfortable and exceptionally joyful at the same time.

Judy, like all the others, wept when she saw the sculpture. What she saw before her was a beautiful expression of love, crafted by this man who had so angered her. She had long since softened toward Ben for not turning over the journal but had resisted taking any step toward reconciliation.

She waited until the crowds had thinned and Ben was no longer in demand. She had seen him look in her direction more than once and blushed each time. She'd spoken to Sunny and found out about the commissioned piece Ben was working on. Finally the two found each other alone alongside the pond.

"It's beautiful, Ben. I had no idea you were an artist."

"Well, thanks. I guess you only knew me as a truck driver and a thief."

"No, I don't. I mean, I did…I guess. But not now. I'm sorry. I'm sorry for what I said and what I did. Now that I've read the journal, I…well, I understand."

Ben looked in her eyes and saw she meant it. "I'm sorry too. I've meant to write you a letter. But I'm just not good with words. Come out to the truck with me. I have something else to give you."

As the two walked side by side around the house, they didn't escape the watchful eye of Skeeter Wilson, who smiled and breathed a prayer of thanksgiving.

Ben was parked almost a block down the street. When they reached his truck, he unlocked it and took out a shoebox. "I knew you'd be here today, and I wanted you to have this."

The box was quite heavy for its size. Judy unfolded its flaps and gasped. She pulled out another bronze, this one about a foot high. It was a barefoot little boy in a tunic, joyfully skipping down the road. On the base were the words of Luke 2:52: "And Jesus grew in wisdom and stature, and in favor with God and men."

She looked up at Ben, her eyes shining bright and wet. "It's beautiful. You made growing up look like a joyful thing."

"I think it's supposed to be."

"I'll treasure it always." Then the new, improved Judy Estes did something that surprised even her. She stood to the tips of her toes and kissed the furry cheek of Ben Shoffner. "Thank you."

They talked for quite a while longer until the girls found them. They made plans to eat together after church the next day, and the late summer afternoon burst forth with the allure of hope and the possibilities of love and joy yet to come.

About the Author

Ed Rowell intentionally lives to help others live intentionally. As a pastor, speaker, and writer, he longs to help people see they were created to make a difference. Living in beautiful Monument, Colorado, with his wife, Susan, and daughters, Melody and Meagan, Ed serves as senior pastor of Tri-Lakes Chapel, a non-denominational church for ordinary people who want to transform the world—one relationship at a time.

Ed accepts a limited number of speaking opportunities each year. If you are interested in having him at your next retreat or conference, go to www.edrowell.com or www.liveintentionally.com for more information.